Stapelia Mixta

Stapelia Mixta

Dr. Mises

Translated by Erik Butler

WAKEFIELD PRESS
CAMBRIDGE, MASSACHUSETTS

Wakefield Press, P.O. Box 425645, Cambridge, MA 02142

Originally published in German as *Stapelia mixta* in 1824.

This book was set in Garamond Premier Pro and Helvetica Neue Pro by Wakefield Press. Printed and bound by Versa Press in the United States of America.

ISBN: 978-1-962728-01-0

Available through D.A.P./Distributed Art Publishers
75 Broad Street, Suite 630
New York, New York 10004
Tel: (212) 627-1999
Fax: (212) 627-9484

10 9 8 7 6 5 4 3 2 1

CONTENTS

TRANSLATOR'S INTRODUCTION

> A man of genius can hardly be sociable, for what dialogues could indeed be so intelligent and entertaining as his own monologues?
>
> Schopenhauer

Right off the bat, this book declares that something stinks. In German, *Dr. Mises* sounds like "Dr. Rotten."[1] *Stapelia mixta* refers to a flower "emitting a fragrance that prompts carrion flies to lay their eggs on it by mistake." The names of the pseudonymous writer and his work seem like a warning meant to shoo off readers. It proves a pleasant surprise, then, to find a garden redolent of learning and wit, tended by a prickly but charming individual.

All the same, one does come to question the latter's intentions.

Dr. Mises is the alter ego of Gustav Theodor Fechner (1801–1887).[2] Even in nineteenth-century Germany, the self-declared "land of poets and thinkers," he stands out for the volume and variety of his work. Fechner's first degree was in medicine. However, he never practiced the profession, preferring to direct his attention toward natural science and philosophy. Writing on everything from landscaping to the spiritual lives of plants and heavenly bodies, Fechner also conducted pioneering research in optics and experimental psychology. He was never not busy; from the age of twenty-two, he lectured at his alma mater in Leipzig and translated scientific works on the side. In 1834, he was appointed full professor (*Ordinarius*) of physics. Concurrently, he oversaw the publication of a "household dictionary" (*Hauslexikon*) in eight volumes numbering close to a thousand pages apiece that covered law, medicine, architecture, animal husbandry, and everything else even remotely pertaining to domestic life; Fechner wrote about a third of the entries himself. In 1839, the strain of constant work left him half-insane and all but blind, forcing him to resign his academic post. Four years later, counter to expectation and probability, he recovered his health and wits. In 1843, still at Leipzig, he was appointed professor of natural philosophy and anthropology—a position he held for the rest of an illustrious and extraordinarily productive career.

Most of Fechner's publications under the Mises moniker appeared before his nervous breakdown: *Proof That the Moon Is Made of Iodine* (1821), *Panegyric of Current Medicine and Natural History* (1822), *Stapelia mixta* (1824), *Comparative Anatomy of Angels* (1825), *Protective Measures for Cholera* (1832), and *Little Book on Life after Death* (1836). *Four Paradoxes* (1846) marks the last time Mises took the public stage.[3] If Fechner did not sign his name to some of his writings, preferring to let another voice speak, this is because "Dr. Rotten" belongs to a turbid, troubled element; he exists only insofar as the author stands at odds with himself and the world. An incarnation of discontent, Mises left the scene when Fechner established an enduring equilibrium in his personal and professional lives.

Mises is a creature of learning run rampant, who presumes to discourse on anything and everything. The sixteen essays in *Stapelia mixta* include discussions of dancing, food, drugs, ancient Greece, the soul and immortality, perception and psychology, the differences and similarities between art, science, and religion, and much more. Ranging in length from a single page to about two dozen, they are erudite romps. When apposite, Mises refers to predecessors and contemporaries, and he is always ready to entertain a counterargument. In the process, he bruits as many opinions he does not hold as opinions he does. By design, the book contains a lot of hot air.

Hot air rises. The last four or five pieces in *Stapelia mixta* swell at heights of abstraction where it is difficult for even Mises himself to breathe. Here, among other things, he proposes to demonstrate the laws governing organic life throughout the cosmos on the basis of geometry. "The circle symbolizes self-love, or egoism, the ellipse the ideal of friendship, the parabola love for the infinite, or divine, and the hyperbola bitterest hatred." Any number of formulas and diagrams are trotted out, but their merit is difficult to gauge: theoretical ambition outstrips practical understanding on every score. Finally, after lengthy elucubrations, Mises declares: "I defer further discussion until a propaedeutic fundament has been achieved." The words hardly herald triumph. The cart stands before the horse—which the driver seems to be pushing.

Self-satire is one of the many darts in Mises's quiver; "Dr. Rotten" pokes plenty of fun at himself and his kind. "On the Dance" and "Encomium of the Belly" mock top-heavy intellectuals while celebrating the feet and stomach, respectively. "Grecomania" and "The Origin of Dew" impersonate Romantic rhapsodists lost in reverie. "On the Classification of Women" and "On Definitions of Life" send up contemporary misogyny and the taxonomies of natural philosophers. (The former, in particular, will shock readers today; it is worth repeating that the piece *does not* reflect the author's views.) And so on, and so on.

There is, for all that, a serious side to the seemingly crackpot ideas. And there is high-mindedness in spite of the self-deprecation. *Stapelia mixta* offers a ludic exploration of topics Fechner would later treat in earnest. In particular, "The Greatest Artist" and "The World Upside Down" point forward to *Zend-Avesta* (1851),[4] the author's most important statement of his views on matters of belief. Borrowing the title of the holy book of Zoroastrianism and claiming to align himself with natural religion of old, Fechner presents his understanding of the entire organic universe as animate, up to and including the planets. This doctrine of panpsychism, which Fechner expounds in mature works, is no less far-fetched than when Mises writes in jest,

> We are simply the particular thoughts in the great brain of God, and we call God's mental images of plants, beasts, and stars real things because we, who call ourselves real too, exist in their company and at their side. Time is the course of God's thoughts, space the delineation of His fantasy, and the cause-and-effect of the material world connections between His ideas. . . . And this God, for whom we are mere thoughts, is Himself but a thought of Himself, of God-greater-still.

In this dispensation, the prevailing law is mental, not moral, as it is in Christianity. God is too alive and omnipresent, vivifying creatures great and small, ever to play the part of judge. "Dr. Rotten" expresses no view that cannot ultimately be reclaimed by Fechner, his dialectical counterpart.

Levity and gravity go together like night and day. Invariably, a "new morning" dispels darkness and gloom, for the two perspectives on reality are not equally valid.[5] More exists than does not, and just because something fades from view does not mean that it ceases to *be*. What is, is both enduring and transformative, investing a new form as it sheds an old one. The life of true sentiment is illustrative: "Hatred will often die with its object, but never love."

The levity in *Stapelia mixta* gets no higher than "Idea for a Higher Culinary Art." Invoking the model provided by musical composition, Mises proposes that substances ranging from spices to narcotics be used to engineer an experience not just for the eyes or ears, but for all the senses:

> One would take first one glass, then another, in the rhythm prescribed by the meal's composer, who had arranged them in keeping with each component's capacity to induce transition from one effect to another or in light of their combined qualities. Thus, seven drops from one vial and three from another would roll over the tongue, followed by a

> teaspoon of powder; one might chew a certain leaf, sniff at a flask, and so on and so forth, until one had eaten one's way through the piece. The finale would come from a substance that brought together the effects of all the others in a chorus of wholesome sentiment.

Mises envisions a synesthetic banquet where one feasts on illusion, some forty years before Charles Baudelaire's *Artificial Paradises* (1860) and approximately one hundred years before surrealist experiments with chemically altered states of consciousness or the futurist project of reinventing cuisine.[6]

From this altitude, it also becomes clear who some of Mises's stylistic and spiritual forebears were. They include Renaissance satirist François Rabelais (ca. 1494–1553) and Jacobean encyclopedist Robert Burton (1577–1640). The books of Rabelais—or "Alcofribas Nasier," as he presented himself to readers anagrammatically—revel in the intoxication afforded by food, drink, and humanist learning. Burton's *Anatomy of Melancholy* (1621) sounds the depths of scholarly despair over hundreds of sprawling pages, but the author calls himself "Democritus Junior" after the ancient philosopher famous for laughing at the absurdity of human existence. An immediate predecessor, to whom Fechner sent copies of the first three books he published as Mises, was humorist Jean Paul (born Johann Paul Friedrich Richter, 1763–1825); in his novels and short stories, this well-respected but riddling writer pushed the art of digression beyond the limits probed by Laurence Sterne (1713–1768) decades earlier in *Tristram Shandy* (1759–1767).

Mises has descendants, too. Diogenes Teufelsdröckh, the philosopher of clothes in Thomas Carlyle's *Sartor Resartus* (1833–1834), is one; his name can be translated as both "devil's print" and "devil's dung." Another is Alfred Jarry's Dr. Faustroll; this *fin de siècle* sage is an exponent of pataphysics, or the science of "laws governing exceptions," and was born at the cranky age of sixty-three.[7] In fact, the hordes of mad scientists that have teemed in literature and film since the late nineteenth century are all, one way or the other, the kinfolk of "Dr. Rotten."

Something unsettling inheres in prodigious learning: the possibility of subterfuge and ruse. Intelligence can always be used for purposes of mystification, and Dr. Mises is not above sleight-of-hand or playing fast and loose with the facts. It can be difficult to unpack the intricacies of his prose, especially since it builds in momentum from word to word, sentence to sentence, and page to page. Patience and attention are required to discern telling shifts in tone and emphasis, and references that are obscure in the twenty-first century would not necessarily have been easier to follow in the nineteenth. *Stapelia mixta* is funny, but "funny" means different things. A joke can be funny, but so can a feeling—in which case the word points to something that's worrisome. As noted, Dr. Mises has relations with a perverse—and even diabolical—sensibility. It is probably not wrong to detect a hint of sulfur in the funny bouquet offered by a funny man.

NOTES

1. *Mises* is pronounced the same way as *mieses*, which is colloquial German for "lousy" or "bad."
2. Biographical information is taken from Michael Heidelberger, *Nature from Within: Gustav Theodor Fechner and His Psychophysical Worldview*, trans. Cynthia Klohr (Pittsburgh: University of Pittsburgh Press, 2004).
3. Decades later, when *Stapelia mixta* was reedited (in *Kleine Schriften* [Leipzig: Breitkopf und Härtel, 1875]), about half the essays were removed and replaced with four new selections. This is one last appearance on Mises's part, if one will; the translation at hand respects the integrity of the original edition.
4. Full title: *Zend Avesta, or On the Heavens and World Beyond from a Naturalistic Standpoint.*
5. Fechner's final exposition of his cosmology, from 1879, translates to "The Day-View Opposed to the Night-View."

6. "Eating futuristically, one uses all the five senses: touch, taste, smell, sight and hearing" (Filippo Tommaso Marinetti, *The Futurist Cookbook*, trans. Suzanne Brill [London: Trefoil, 1989], 77).

7. Alfred Jarry, *Exploits & Opinions of Dr. Faustroll, Pataphysician*, trans. Simon Watson Taylor (Cambridge, MA: Exact Change, 1996), 21, 7.

Stapelia Mixta

FOREWORD

—or, in fact, Afterword, to the title page.

I wanted my book, which is written for the broader public, to go along with fashion and therefore wished to christen it with the name of a flower. Hereby I encountered no small embarrassment. If there's nothing new about a book, at least the title should be. The names of almost all of Flora's children that I knew already adorned other works. A study on which a famous scientist is now working, an excerpt from a botanical system for writers, had not appeared yet; and moreover, no one could guarantee me, no green thumb in the garden of *belles lettres*, that a flower I deemed virginal had not already been married by pen to paper. What to do? Fortunately, I recalled reading once, in *Becker's Almanac*, advice for people who do not wish their children to have the same names as others. "Name your son Judas Iscariot," it said. That very moment, my gaze fell on an exemplar of *stapelia mixta* standing in the window, a flower of somber hue dotted with loud, colored spots and emitting a fragrance that prompts carrion flies to lay their eggs on it by mistake. It occurred to me that just as no Christian would ever name a child Judas Iscariot, so, too, would no writer of fragrant prose be inclined to call his work by the name of a flower like that. My doubts vanished.

May the carrion flies do as they will.

ON THE DANCE

Dance comes first among the arts not just on earth, but throughout the whole world. Indeed, it's as if the horn of Oberon had sounded at Creation for the entire universe, to set it spinning in perpetual cycles. Each planet performs its steps as best it is able, and even the sun, which, on account of its corpulence, cannot be expected to move too much, is swept along by the gay motion and turns on its axis. As far as our own earth is concerned, the *pas de deux* it performs with the moon in the oval, starlit ballroom incontestably gave rise to the waltz, which one therefore is fully entitled to call a heavenly dance. Hold to these bright examples, and let the moralists and doctors who condemn dancing prattle—the former because, if they usually recognize good customs with their heads, they do so all the worse with their withered feet, and the latter because they see only too well that dancing provides the sole means for us to remain healthy in body and soul by following the designs of nature, and that deprives them of their livelihood. Doesn't their own science of anatomy teach that the foot, by its very form, is made for nothing but dancing, how one muscle seems built for the *pas glissé*, another for the *pas floré*, and so on? That as many kinds of step must exist as there are muscles in the legs; that man has toes and an arch to rise up and extend the foot appropriately; that he is endowed with cushiony calf muscles (or, at any rate, a place to install artificial ones) to avoid self-injury when executing *entrechats*; and that nerves run through all these muscles so they can launch into the proper convulsions as soon as a note is struck on the violin? Doctors know there's nothing to gain from someone dancing, who prefers downing a glass of punch or lemonade all at once to taking "a teaspoon every two hours" from a bottle; that's why they seek out places where people creep around like shadows or listlessly lie abed. Here, Nature is avenging herself upon those who disregard her will. Why aren't these fools dancing? Then they wouldn't be sick or dead. After all, there's nothing more invigorating than a brisk waltz to a well-played fiddle. Anyone biased against dancing should just imagine, when observing a ball, that people who have sat themselves sick all week are now working up a sweat and getting their circulation going, with one or the other participant occasionally striking out feet and arms left and right for the sake of well-being; then he will find the utility plain.

For my part, I would rather be a wooden top spun with a strap by a boy, like the musician whipping us to dance with his bow, than a sapient scholar whose appendages do nothing more than give the chair he occupies six wooden legs instead of four. This is also why, of all shapes, the sphere displays the most perfect form: it has an infinite number of limbs for dancing and indeed consists of nothing but them; for each point is a tiptoe around which it can, and really does, spin at the slightest push. We, imperfect beings that we are, possess only two such points, which a sage of antiquity called divine, by means of which we emulate the circling paths of the heavens. These organs are also the noblest part of our whole body; just as two consuls once bore the burden of the Roman state, it is these limbs' office to preserve, steer, and govern the organism, which must needs ply to their will. Just as the clumsy head of a needle exists for the sake of the point alone, so too does the human head have value only in relation to the feet, inasmuch as it directly or indirectly promotes their art.

No deep comparison is required to arrive at the insight that the art of dance occupies a station above all others. One stands just five minutes before a painting, exclaims "Beautiful!" and then, later on, tells one's friends that one spent a whole hour admiring it. But has anyone ever left a ball before nightfall has given way to sunrise without declaring that time has flown by?—Why is music practiced with such zeal, if not to show that lovely hands can dance on keys just as well as feet on the floor? Why have artists devoted themselves to studying harmony but to write great operas from which waltzes and polkas might be derived? Indeed, we can affirm that the hallmark of good music is that it lends itself to this purpose. Who, among the elegant set, attends a concert but to find an engagement there for the next ball? Or, if it really strikes one's fancy, it's that one knows, or one's ear senses, below the threshold of consciousness, that the notes consist of the tiniest particles executing exquisite movements (figures of sound), such as only the greatest of human dancers can perform, so a composer actually should be deemed a dancing master who brings order and harmony to corporeal elements that would otherwise simply be hopping about. Who has not, by the third hour of a concert (if not the second, or even the first), taken out his pocket watch many times, yearning for the intermission—an oasis in the desert, as it were, offering tea and sorbet—just to speak, at long last, a sensible word after all the sawing of strings and puffing of flutes? Whose ears are not quick to hand over the ticket of admission to the eyes, and who has not experienced mortal *ennui* upon realizing that his own bouquet does not lie under the stage lights among the colorful offerings? In contrast, is there anyone who has ever removed his hand from a slender waist to hide a yawn? What man with properly functioning feet would hesitate to choose between a symphony by Beethoven and a jig, between nodding along to airy harmonies and cutting elegant shapes on the floor? Who would not willingly ooze sweat from every pore like the barrel of the Danaids, coughing, groaning, and working himself into a lather fit to inspire compassion in any onlooker ignorant of the art? And one does it all without any recompense; dust and wax get all over one's clothes, shoes are scratched up and worn down, and every last piece of white is rendered black and sooty; when the sweat's gone, one spits and there's the tang of blood in the nose and mouth—and all for nothing, nothing at all. Only the inner dignity of the dance can account for willingly subjecting oneself to such hardship. It is only right, then, that dancing be considered an ascent to heavenly, nay godly, heights, as the human striving to partake of angelic existence: we think we have wings and want to fly, but in the end it's mere jumping around, since the burden of our earthly frame drags us back down. Never content with just one attempt, one endeavors to soar until spent; a few have found paradise already by striving for the same.

The art of dance would really be ashamed at comparison with the art of poetry today. Leaving aside the fact that the former makes its entry on two balanced feet, whereas the latter hobbles along on one long foot and another short one, dancing is a free art; poetry, on the other hand, is practiced for the sake of earning a living—whereby, if only in passing, let me say that I am amazed the guild has failed to keep up with the level of culture and professional self-esteem demonstrated by other trades; for instance, a tailor now wants to be known as a designer; the poet ought to style himself as a maker-of-verses and hang a sign outside the door so clients will know that he accommodates all wishes, made-to-measure; such a display might feature Apollo, the patron of the art, in silhouette: a figure of skin and bones fishing with his lyre for a side of bacon, strumming at a wedding for a piece of the cake, or seasoning his soup with the leaves of his laurels; Bacchus and Silenus are painted in this manner at taverns, and their likeness might even pass for that of Apollo, who has dismounted from Pegasus once and for all; Bacchus is often portrayed astride a barrel of wine, behaving as unmannerly as if he had drunk it all at once and shooting a jet of the clearest water.—

Well did the ancient Greeks know that that there is no better way to celebrate days holy to the gods than with "graceful, winding, soulful dance about the refulgent altar." It's basically no different in our own day: ball-day is a holiday, and the whole week—especially the higher one goes among the educated classes—amounts to preparation for the same; only now, matters aren't divided so neatly; instead of dancing around the altar, as before, pious souls (inasmuch as there are no outstanding arrangements to be made for what really counts: the ball itself) take a seat at the altar in the morning and reverently consider the coming evening, when the dancing takes place without it; the altar no longer need serve as the station for censers of incense and myrrh, when every participant at the festivities exudes a scent of his or her own; plus, want of space often demands that room be left for the buffet. The dances of the Greeks likely possessed a character wholly different from those today. That ancient people did not know waltzing at all, just as, in general, their lives and thinking revolved around the objective world instead of the subjective one so dear to us: people now consider themselves the center of the universe and move on their own axis, as occurs in the waltz. When I hear that the Greeks—and

Greek ladies in particular—were ignorant of this dance, I can only marvel in the manner of the Hindu learning that life in England is possible even though the land possesses no coconuts.

There's no denying that the fair sex excels in the sense of beauty—its own, especially—such that, in our estimate of the art of dance, we must grant women the right of way. It's true that men are happy to take a spin, but we also like to hunt, ride, and fence. For a girl, however, nothing surpasses the waltz, including the new dress she's wearing; I'm convinced that any one of them would gladly sacrifice one of her feet if doing so meant she had permission to dance with the other; after all, many a girl devotes her life to the waltz to such an extent that the phrase, "I'm dying to dance," can be taken literally. Indeed, I remember reading, in Passavant's *Lebensmagnetismus*, of young ladies who could barely lift a finger to do anything under normal circumstances but would spin around for hours, without ever getting tired, just as soon as it was a matter of dancing.

See how well-mannered that girl sitting there is: she would appear to be little more than an artful lever for setting knitting needles into motion. At each gaze cast her way, she retreats into her shell, darting a cautious glance like antennae only after a stretch of time, to make sure no stumbling block lies in her path; give her a little poke, and off she scoots, as if a spider had landed on her; watch her gait: like she's taking a tiny ant for a walk and has sworn by St. Andrew that she will never allow the tip of one delicate foot to see the heel of the other. Now behold this work of subtle, feminine machinery at a ball: dance alone infuses her with life and soul. Her step strides all on its own, striking the floor to the music at the very first round, like a warhorse champing at the bit when the trumpet blows, furious at the reins holding it back; see how the formerly docile creature pours herself into a commanding embrace, muscles rippling like the stormy sea, eyes ablaze and casting sparks in the frenzy of alien gazes; word, deed, and each glance that she casts make it clear that she belongs to a higher, nobler sphere. And is this not what the ball is? Aren't the title "goddess" and "angel" as universal here as that of *citoyenne* in any republic? Isn't everyone a flower without scent that now begins to waft a heady fragrance in spite of all the cologne and perfume? Don't every man and woman cast off mortal flesh to be reborn in a new and transfigured body in the heaven of the ballroom? Aren't the aged rejuvenated and withered life renewed as wrinkles transform into furrows where carmine-red roses are planted and grow? The hair and gown of each lady burst into flower, men without locks (or even hair at all) erupt in bloom, and the skinniest legs burgeon with shapely calves. Here, what seemed impossible becomes reality; a foot the size of camel's fits into the needle's eye of a doll's shoe; a bumblebee's midriff is squeezed into the waist of a wasp; a nagging mouth beams an angel's smile; stone-cold hearts, never to be moved by tears, melt in the sticky goo of warm sentiment; the dingiest Cinderella struts about like an alabaster princess; apprentices condemned to toil in perpetual squatting shoot forth handsome limbs; instead of compounded medicines, the pharmacist distributes sweet words, glances, and candies. No one would mistake it for day-to-day life on earth!

It is little wonder why, for many beauties, summer is the saddest time of year, for it puts an end to the ball season; true, there are the joys of nature—yet how little do they make up for what has been lost. Dawn may well be majestic, but the sun makes a point of rising earlier than we do, peeking through the window at our ladies as they go about their *toilette* while preserving its own modesty; and it's equally wicked at dusk, setting just as the ladies, out on a stroll, are in the middle of debating the merits of a hat, shoe, or other article of finery so they can't see what they're talking about. Although lovely flowers grow in summertime, they do so at places visited primarily by sheep and cows; in contrast, where human beings deambulate, there's more dust from the road than pollen from plants. What, then, does summer provide that could take the place of the winter pastime of dancing? At most, summer is to be viewed as a weak effort on the part of nature to compensate us a little bit for being deprived of dancing and give us time to rally our forces for later; as such, it deserves our gratitude. The sun only seems so hot at this time of year because the human constitution relies on a daily evacuation of sweat by means of dancing—which, in physiological terms, effects much the same as pushing and squeezing out waste in other forms of elimination—and during the summer, when people need to rest, perspiration would come to a halt without beneficent intervention. Surely the biblical phrase, "By the sweat of your brow you will eat your food," means that one shouldn't dine before dancing.

Were one blind as a bat to their merits, one would still have to admit that balls bestir the industriousness of young ladies. Many a girl who would otherwise not deign to touch a needle and instead keeps her hands folded in her lap, is roused to the busy practice of art, fingers flying as the ball approaches just as fast as her feet soon will move. For eight days beforehand, then mentally for eight days afterward, she thrives: the period between one ball and the next qualifies as a time of plowing and sowing, or enjoying the fruits of the harvest—the pleasure of fond recollection and, still more, talking about the event.

Consider the artist who, for weeks on end, has been carrying around the idea for a canvas; he sets out to procure the best material and most brilliant paints; then, practically forgetting to eat or drink, he remains planted at the easel, immersed in schemes to carry out the design that will be his crowning glory when the exhibition opens; over and over, hundreds of times, he reworks what he has done and touches up details, never quite attaining the vision in his mind—a divine conception that, he is quite certain, will make visitors pass by other paintings and remain standing before his alone. Now, instead of a painter, picture a girl, with a mirror in place of the easel, needles and scissors instead of brushes, and youthful appreciation of all one's charms in lieu of artistic schemes; that's the very image of a young lady preparing for a Christmas ball or other dance on a grand scale.

May the good Lord forgive fathers and mothers so tyrannical they would deny their daughters attendance at such an event; undoubtedly, far more girls have died from grief at missing a ball than have expired on the dance floor; and even if one or two of them have become consumptive after a night out, isn't it far lovelier to dance breezily from this life than to creep out, hunched and bent over, having long since planted one foot in the grave? When a man falls at war, he is said to rest on a "bed of honor." Well, it's the same here: a valiant girl, if fated to die by dancing, will stare the reaper himself in the eye with as much courage as a warrior on the field; at most, she'll ask for a reprieve for one more waltz.

Likewise, I declare those mothers inhuman who coo as they drag balking daughters off the ballroom floor before the cock has crowed that it's time for the night watchman to retire. Barbarians! Are you unmoved by the imploring gaze of your child, who pleads so sweetly?—"It's not good for your health, my dear, that's enough for today."—"You wanted to go as soon as I started having fun."—"Now, now, I've been tired for hours, and look, your father will get mad."—"Just the cotillion, then I'll be glad to go."—"Not another waltz for you, you need rest; you're getting carried away. You'll thank me tomorrow." And lo, flutes and violins beckon the couples to a cheery round. The girl's foot is moving with a will of its own. Just then, the most dashing gentleman of the assembly blows in like a zephyr on tiptoe: "Charming young lady, may I be so bold?"—But the poor girl must refuse. Sobbing within, she looks on at the shimmering dance, as her suitor drifts away with another. Sullenly, she puts on her scarf and pouts all the way home. The couples close ranks like waves, a tide surging up and down; the luckless girl will never see a single one of them again.

GRECOMANIA

The ancient Greeks transcribed nature, whose grand characters must be drawn in slow and deliberate traits, not a brisk, cursive scrawl; therefore, they also had few books, but good ones for the main. A tree that brings forth myriad fruits generally yields an insipid and sour crop, just as a flower often loses its lovely fragrance, its very spirit, in the process of blooming. For the Greeks, thoughts were living beings that donned the attire of words so they might be introduced among human beings, and this adornment was something beautifully Greek. In contrast, what is written today presents marionettes, which are supposed to learn to ape life through dress and outward embellishment; these figures do not move on their own, and each step reveals the string with which the author modulates the gestures they perform. Just as the torso must now conform to the corset—a pathological health-contraption from which long life is hoped, but not obtained—modern poetry is determined by mere verbal attire, verse by rhyme; yet by this means the author would achieve immortality! The same hand wielded bow and lyre among the Greeks, and the sound of the first echoed in the second; each and every word was authored by a deed and a child of the same. We, on the other hand, learn what we are to do in the first place from books. Each painting made by the Greeks bore the imprint of nature's engraving, whereas we copy one plate from another; that is why their works are so vivid and ours so dim. Among the Greeks, the shades of the departed thought and acted as if they were still alive; likewise, words were adumbrations of true life—not a copy so much as a continuation. Our books show another world, into which characters have been placed and which has little in common with the one here. When we set out to depict the heavens, effort yields a vague, blue haze with a few smooth, angelic visages peeking out, as if simply to declare, "This is the sky." But the Greeks painted the blessed themselves, and thus the heavens emerged on their own. Greek similes grafted only related stock to a trunk, which is why their images have been able to perpetuate and renew themselves up to the present day. Our wit tends to come out as a minotaur combining wholly dissimilar elements in a baroque monster to be marveled at but once—and then, afterward, banished as a misshapen abomination. The ancients always borrowed their images from human life or nature, gathering what the latter spontaneously brought forth to adorn their allegories, whereas we consider natural flowers altogether too ordinary and therefore fashion artificial ones; they fool the senses from afar, but up close, lacking a spiritual fragrance, they reveal themselves to be dead assemblages. In general, natural things show themselves to be even more beautiful and radiant when contemplated through a microscope, whereas artificial ones only lose luster and charm; so too do the writings of the Greeks—men who might be deemed the instruments of nature—cast a greater light upon inspection, while modern works, which shine mainly because of the varnish applied, prove cheap and unprepossessing.

To run pure and clear, Aganippe didn't need to pass through the filter of a thousand aesthetic precepts; just as the Greeks, ignoring corsets and girdles, grew up handsome and tall with divinity dwelling in their breasts, so too did their poetry spring forth from inner fullness, instinctively exemplifying the rules of art, in floral sprays turned toward the sun of beauty and truth. Indeed, are not most of the rules we observe today born of their verse? But the verdant branch now is used simply for measuring, if not as a ruler for striking the knuckles, and it is unable to bring forth new bloom. The works of antiquity are immortal gods, destined to live perpetually, beyond time, on the heights of Parnassus, Helicon, Olympus, and Ida; even though our own writings are descended from them, they are mere mortals; like the leaves of trees—*hôste phylla dendrôn*—they grow only to wither and fall.

Indeed, is this still the same heavenly muse, a goddess, who descended to bring poets her art and make herself understood to human beings? Is this the same muse, sunken to unbecoming infatuation, who now offers herself to the lowest of the low? For isn't it often the case that an author writes simply because his stomach is empty, not because his heart is full? Gout or sloth has bound him to the chair, and he drains his boredom onto the page, which begets equally unattractive spawn in the reader. Pegasus once bore the spirit aloft on bold wings, drawing close to the god of light and poetry and disclosing a fairer view of the world below. But poets are like olives. Good oil is coaxed forth by the beams of the radiant sun god and flows on its own from ripe fruit; what's pressed out by necessity is bitter. Nor should the poet strive for the green branches crowning the palm. A laurel wreath was enough for the song of the ancient Greeks, and they were happy to pass on to others the gifts of the muse. Her bequest was not weighed and traded, as it were; vigorous conception and execution weren't thinned down, like milk, with water for gain, husks and chaff cast among the grain just to fill the bushel. The Greek sowed the uncorrupted seeds from the hand of the goddess freely, and so we still enjoy the majestic harvest, which could never have grown if choked by weeds.

Mercury has again snatched from Apollo the lyre that once, according to legend, he gave him in unblemished state. Struck by unskilled hands, it has fallen out of tune and emits rough, unmelodious tones. If the strings weren't made of gold, the god of wheeling and dealing would simply throw the lovely instrument into the trash.

ENCOMIUM OF THE BELLY

Man, in general, does not sufficiently appreciate what a noble part of himself his belly is; but it's the way of the world that true merit should be recognized only after the fact: the belly is assigned a station below the brain and heart, which eat its bread and drink its wine, and then make fun of it. To be sure, the brain stuffs people full of well-turned phrases, but ultimately there's nothing behind them; the stomach, however, like a quiet wise man, guards silence and promotes general well-being all the more for so doing; and like the sun, which shines over good and evil alike, it shares its bounty with the limbs contemning it, which, were it but to stay its gentle hand, would soon abandon their insolent ways. Indeed, the Pegasus that is the brain would drop its wings in submission if the belly did not provide oats at the right time. The whole body is, in fact, an excrescence of the stomach, wrapped around it like a shell or pelt to keep it soft and warm; this shell would lie dead and useless if the nutmeat of the belly were not there. To remove the belly from man would be like taking the queen from the hive; not a limb would stir, for who would there be to serve? *Plenus venter non studet libenter*, the proverb rightly goes, because the mind is not allowed to disturb the belly with its trifles when the latter is engaged in serious business; it would be ten times more true, then, that a *vacuus venter*—in other words, a stomach without anything in it—would not study at all. Whatever the human head brings forth is like a fly's spittle: ooze for collecting more food to feed the belly.

Of course, there have been philosophers who have endeavored to demean the stomach in various ways, considering it a kind of bubble within the pure glass of human being that distorts spiritual reflections; however, these are mostly people who haven't had much to stick in their own guts and have therefore considered the belly a bag in want of the proper filling; they ought to consider that all the mental efflorescence of which they boast sprouts from here and therefore amounts to little more than a sublimated belch that, instead of issuing from the gullet, has, through a series of vessels and nerves acting as so many filters, cast off its grosser form to peek out of the brain without corporeal integument.

True, the stomach may not fancy itself much, but why should it rack its wits? After all, the brain is a laborer working its fields, where grow lovely ideas, poetry, philosophy, and other bountiful plants; the latter may show fair blossoms, but they bear real fruit only through manifold transubstantiations into bread, meat, and beer—wine rarely enters the picture in this particular branch of culture—for the use and benefit of the belly, which in turn apportions the day's wages to the brain. If the kind of person usually called a "bad apple" wants to grumble, it amounts to about as much as a starving artist thinking himself above the owner of the building because his lowly garret is on the top floor: he's still happy for crumbs from the table.

Hunger is the best cook, to whom we owe our most sublimated, rarefied, and spiritual pleasures; it's the whip with which the belly rouses the mind to work; when the former is at rest, the latter just crawls off to lie down—or actually falls asleep. A hungry person can do anything, while one who is sated does nothing at all; the first will muster all he can to achieve the goals of life in this world, and the second has already done so; this is why a celebrated natural philosopher has declared that hunger is thought itself: perforce, first principles determine final ends.

In fact, our whole culture is the product of gastric activity. The stomach is an egg from which all the arts and sciences are hatched; were it no longer to let things through, all cultural advancement would be over and done: having eaten one's fill, further efforts would cease and the world would stagnate in a gloomy *farniente*; as it stands, the belly cheerfully takes in all that is offered, shows whatever has outstayed its welcome the back door, and then turns to greet other—and often worthier—guests; in this way, man is ever roused to new endeavor. A poet who has buttered his bread with an ode to immortality still stands in obligation to his belly and must enlist its aid to get a few ideas about love, friendship, or whatever else it is that happens to be selling at the moment; to enjoy better fare, some poets endeavor to write better works; others, lacking the talent to fill their stomach in any other way, take up poetry in the first place just for a bite. The belly might be shown to exercise a similar influence elsewhere. Instead of nine muses, it would be better to picture nine stomachs; their attributes might include the most delectable dishes from each province of nature. The sight of the same would be sufficiently mouthwatering to inspire great artistic efforts, if only for the sake of satisfying one's appetite after the fact; yet as it stands, the muses are painted with things like lyres and other instruments, welcome side dishes at a thoughtfully arranged table, but hardly suited to fan the fires of fantasy. Just set, before a poetaster, the most splendid poem on one plate and a roll with fatty sardines on another; he will surely reach for the first—to wipe off his greasy fingers. The loveliest verse leaves most people cold, but who doesn't warm up at the very thought of hot soup?—In antiquity, meals were accompanied by recitations. This was a sign of humanistic refinement, since it meant allowing the brain, a mere servant, to dine with its master, the belly; in contrast, recitations in our own day are attended by frequent opening of the mouth, which seems to signal the desire to fill the stomach. Verses that are perfectly good often serve to wrap up cheese, which is even better fare; but no cheese is ever used to pack up a poem: it is unseemly to demean something noble by putting it in service to baser matter.

The noontime meal forms the center of life, and it does so each and every day; here, all the rays of vital activity converge, coming to rest and then shooting forth again. The periods between breakfast, lunch, and dinner could be omitted entirely, were it not that humans need time to work up an appetite. The most spiritual of beings may be pictured as an infinite belly that never eats its fill and is always ready for more. Needless to say, few of us mortal, imperfect creatures can attain such blessedness, even in approximate fashion; we'd have to be tubes with food ever passing from one end to the other; but that's also what sets us apart from polyps, which aren't much more than bags. Man is equipped with an array of artfully designed appendages to feed the stomach, of which the mind is the cleverest: under the cover of seeming idleness, it prowls for the belly better than any limb.

The belly is the alpha and omega of Creation; the lowest sort of animals, *infusoria*, are a stomach and nothing else; the highest order of creature, according to the most recent findings, at any rate, are simply compounded versions of the same: *infusoria* to the *n*th power, with intricate stomachs taking in air, sounds, light, and other stuff, all of them performing functions per the instructions of the Grand Stomach (the governmental seat, so to speak). Upon entering the world, the human being wants to eat; upon departure, it is eaten. A general devouring pervades and sustains the world, which is one vast belly consuming and, in so doing, nourishing itself; its sustenance consists of lesser bellies that are digesting and being digested in turn. Minerals eat their fill of oxygen in the air and water; to their innermost atom, they are bellies, and once sated, they know of nothing better to do than lie there lifeless until meal-time, when they bring forth light and warmth—confirming our statement above, that all activity in this world is based on digestion, and hunger the very soul of the world, which otherwise would be as inert as a rock. Plants eat away at stone and open their gullets to swallow light; yet nature does not gladly give away so much at once from her larder, and thus she draws it away from vegetation through myriad pores; as such, the life of plants is basically an ongoing feud with nature for their daily bread. In turn, animals devour plants, and human beings animals; essentially, however, the opposite is also true: if we can say that the Creator has made plants for the stomachs of man and beast, it is equally demonstrable that man and beast are simply bundles of matter to be loosened up and prepared, through organic processes, for the highest and ultimate end: to rot and provide rich piles of fertilizer for plants.

Even the fact that almost all illnesses derive from the stomach or its immediate surroundings offers proof of its perfection; saying so seems contradictory at first, yet it is altogether natural that the slightest inconvenience in a noble organ of our body should entail disadvantage for the rest of our organism, and do so in more conspicuous fashion than problems besetting a lesser part; accordingly, we can observe how all our thoughts sometimes seem jumbled, when fantasy has metastasized in the faculty of understanding or reason; the craziest things go on in our heads, and the rest of the body barely seems to notice. True, bodily functions involve the extraction of thoughts by processing the materials the senses provide; theoretically, one might posit that the body suffers when the brain does not adequately command this form of secretion. But many organs can take over the job of other parts when things aren't working properly. This is the case for the tasks of the brain. If a person isn't right in the head, he might relieve himself more frequently, sweat a little more, get a nosebleed, or something like that; hereby the utility that thinking supposedly offers the organism is compensated in full. The same does not hold for the operations of the stomach, which cannot be handed over to just any other organ. Only the belly knows how to preside over them; when it is indisposed, the whole organism sounds the alarm and worries for its chieftain and itself: bitter and disaffected, the tongue dons a white mantle and scorns even the sweetest morsels of consolation; as much as possible, the head seeks to relieve the stomach's woes by taking on its pain and dizziness, refusing to think of anything else; fearfully, the blood races this way and that, and the whole system languishes gloomily.

Love might be thought to represent a flight toward higher things that does not require the stomach to provide buoyancy in the manner of a balloon. Upon closer inspection, however, love reveals itself as a developmental illness of adolescence, like teething in small children, that takes the shape of fantasies often exacerbated by moonlight; it is best treated homeopathically, i.e., by the same means that caused the problem in the first place. In physiological terms, love is good for nothing more than promoting an increased level of fat, since the stomach, as it advances in age, does not like to rest on just skin and bones; indeed, fat starts building up as soon as the age of amorous exploits comes to an end—which evidently provides human beings a suitable interval for generating this substance; accordingly, those who tend by nature toward corpulence usually display less pronounced symptoms.

Moreover, since at least Mesmer's time, everyone has known that the belly, if only it wants to, can be the most learned, most ingenious, most philosophical, most poetic, most religious (and so on, and so on) being of all. Doesn't the somnambulist's gut sense penetrate regions denied to mere understanding, boldly soaring over mountains before which the mind stands helpless? Doesn't it see, hear, smell, feel and taste—as if, from childhood on, it had done nothing else—more fully than our ordinary senses, even though that's their job? So great is the belly's inborn genius.

Therefore, O Belly, King and Father and Preserver of the Flesh, be praised! From thine abundant source all in our organism that creeps and courses, grows and thrives, draws its force. Thy hand apportions the bounty, that each member may be content, according to its labors and its needs. Thy working lies hidden, yet thy works are manifest. All that is in and for us, is from thee, indeed our very spirit—every thought and vision and dream—reflects thy majesty, endeavoring to imitate thine action in its own sphere. May we never forget our debt and devote every thought and deed to thy service.

BUT THE GRAVE IS NOT DEEP; IT IS THE RADIANT FOOTSTEP OF AN ANGEL SEEKING US OUT.

Jean Paul

Our true love for another human being often starts when this individual has departed from us; two hearts that have grown together do not always recognize how closely they are knit until death has torn them asunder and the one left behind comes to know by the pain and blood still flowing from the wound. Hatred will often die with its object, but never love. Just as gold shines forth when the lazy slag has been melted away, so too does the departed stand transfigured before our eyes after sloughing off the bodily husk; in the night of death, we make out constellations that we failed to see, or neglected, in the daytime of life. While rooted in human existence, the flower of renown does not burst into the light before one has vanished into darkness. Only from the ashes does it shoot up in splendor and then renew itself a thousandfold, from generation to generation. Before a man has died, he cannot be sure of his immortality; no soul ever joined the divine assembly on Olympus before journeying to Hades; the slings and arrows of disfavor and calumny do not stop their wounding until one has bathed in the River Styx.

But tell me: What use is it to us if the incense of fame embalms us into a mummy for hundreds of years when, in the end, it falls to bits? It's no help to the flower if fragrance persists after its bloom has wilted, nor does it avail the string if the note that breaks it continues to ring; it has been torn from the instrument and will never sound forth in melody again. When the Fates cut the thread of life, they sever the nerves of sensation and sentiment, which tie us to the rest of nature. Truly, our heart is wounded by the thorns of life; but once we have slowly bled to death, we cannot appreciate the roses planted on our grave. Life provokes hot tears among the living, but none of the tears shed at our tomb will break the hard ice with which death immures our heart, nor let us know we are still loved. If an upstanding man—who, while alive, perhaps did not have a place to lay his head—is built a majestic temple, what good does it do him that others now admire it? His own part is just the small, dark chamber of death.

Shouldn't we strike our breasts when we see how death, in gathering the flowers of the earth, too often reaches for the loveliest ones, depriving the world of the best seeds that might yet be sown? We look on as all that is beautiful and sublime dashes toward the abyss from which no steps lead back, the chasm that devours millennia and gives birth only to fleeting instants. Death roams abroad with terrifying calm; its icy finger touches the warm heart of the youth, freezing wishes, hopes, and dreams; the youth's angel goes forth in tears and extinguishes the flame, but death coldly casts the corpse on the field, from which nothing will grow, and goes on its way, taking the budding child from the arms of the despairing mother, who presses one last kiss on pale lips; the waves have barely washed it up from the waters of infinity onto the shining shore of life before the babe is flung back into the gulf of destruction and eternal night, never to rise again. Death's table is decay, and its mead the tears of grieving mothers and brides. Its great black shadow descends on the morning, growing larger and larger until it swallows the sun itself and enshrouds the starry skies; it stands before our hopes for the paradise of a better life, a minatory specter, and we shudder to approach the gates; who can really say that the dusky portal leads to a garden bathed in eternal light, that the black angel of destruction is the guardian for the abode of angels of light and blessed souls?

When the roses on our lips and cheeks are stripped of bloom, when the wilted eye no longer thirsts for light and the rays that strike it are no longer greeted by thoughts that carry them to the innermost soul, when the ear, the tiny echo chamber of the universe, no longer offers strings on which music might sound, when the warmth of life no longer rouses the veins to beat a pulse and their waxing and waning stalls because the heavenly bodies of the flesh have stopped shining, when the tears and smiles of those dear to us cannot bestir sympathy on a face grown pale—isn't it true that the wings are gone that once bore us, mere clay infused with life, above the ashes and dust? Isn't it true that earthly matter now takes its awful revenge on children briefly suffered to make sport on a vibrant island, who thought themselves its rulers but are now taken in its terrible embrace and crushed?

But silence! Why do you hesitate and doubt? Why remain standing at the night that follows the day? A new morning will follow. When you reach the gloomy banks of Acheron and cannot see a shore where your bark might land, hold fast to a star. The star of belief is sure to guide you to the Elysian Fields, where Psyche grows wings of which she will never be robbed.

THE ORIGIN OF DEW

Chloris created the flower, fitted her out with a garment dipped in the luminous rainbow, gave her ethereal light to drink, placed her in the lap of the universal mother, and said: "Let my child want for nothing!" The flower felt the bliss of existence and tilted her delicate head to the earth, as if meditating how to express her gratitude. Then, as the goddess bent over her once more, contentedly contemplating her fine form and taking pleasure in what she had wrought, behold, the flower lifted her crown, spreading a cheerful calyx; sweet fragrances rose up in offering, which the flower had secretly prepared from the clear light that Chloris had given her to drink, along with the purest nectars of the earth. The goddess understood the grateful language of the little blossom, and her heart was moved. A limpid token of joy fell from her eye on the blossoming leaves. The flower enclosed it in her chalice. Still now, she preserves it like a pearl with which she adorns each new day; the auspicious dew has come from rapturous tears.

ON THE CLASSIFICATION OF WOMEN

A Pasquinade

According to recent scholarly accounts, the human being would seem to be nothing but an artful pâté, the masterpiece that nature's Great Cook has compounded from the flesh of all other beasts so that no particular flavor predominates. It's just that the dish isn't quite as successful in the case of woman, for a discerning palate will taste a few elements quite well: dove eyes and a serpent's heart, tongue of magpie, blood of cat, and so forth. Accordingly, debate persists whether woman, in all respects, should really count as a human being, and the previous century witnessed the public defense of a learned dissertation affirming the contrary on the strength of the Bible. Incontestably, the question is weighty, since it cannot be indifferent to man whether he has an actual, if somewhat botched specimen of humanity at his side (as per *Okens Naturphilosophie*, p. 2375, for instance), or a somewhat affected and headstrong domestic animal which, for all that, is indispensable for maintaining a household and may not be mistreated because of a weak constitution and propensity to lapse into a kind of *diabetes lacrymalis*; even though, when one considers how they are built, one is all but forced, by teleological reason, to conclude that men are destined to deal blows and women to receive them passively; clearly, in the former, bones and muscles are the instruments by which force is expressed, while in the latter a padding of fat predominates, which renders too much of the same harmless; this relationship is evident, *in praxi,* among all peoples that still bear a stamp of the natural order.

Indeed, the history of languages and peoples provides great instruction on this score. Almost all languages harbor traces that the predicate *human* has only been assigned to the man with certainty until now. I need only point to French, which has no word for human being other than *homme,* which means, without a doubt, that the man is deemed exemplary of the race; had risk of misunderstanding existed, a special word would easily have been found. In German too, where *Mensch* refers to both sexes, it seems an unconscious need gave rise to the distinction between woman and a true human being, or man. (Therefore, the neutral article *das* precedes the word when applied to a woman.) Such evidence, which occurs in other languages, is significant in itself, since the linguistic genius preserves the first and inborn notions of the human race most purely. However—and over and above all this—positive fact demonstrates the enormous gulf separating human beings and women since time immemorial. Of countless possible proofs, I will adduce only a few. Among the Indians in Guyana, when the man goes on the hunt, the woman must carry the dogs along, so the poor beasts won't get tired; and if they are still young, she must also nurse them on the way.—In Loango, a woman must kneel when speaking to a man.—In Persia, the ladies are excluded from poetry. The Persians say: If a hen wants to crow, her throat needs to be cut.—Among the Samoyeds, not only are women not permitted to eat at the same table as a man; with the exception of rare evenings of tenderness, the latter will not even speak with them, telling them what they need to know with the eyes alone.—In the southern half of Africa, many chiefs and princes keep whole flocks of young girls, in the manner of lambs, cows, and other animals, and are always having a few slaughtered for the table.—Among some Oriental peoples, a man forced to mention his wife or daughter will ask for pardon, or offer some formula of excuse, as we do when discussing matters about which one does not like to speak.—The rabbis say that in the beginning, God created Adam with a long tail; later, upon closer inspection, He decided man would look better without it. So nothing of what He had made would go missing, He cut off the tail and fashioned another creature from it, hence the lower and baser nature of the female sex.

As mentioned, that is just an indication of how the issue has been viewed to date; a more thorough examination, which is proposed here, of the position to assign woman relative to human being demands direct investigation of woman herself. Two approaches are available, starting from either the physical or the psychical side of the female. Here, the question promptly arises whether woman really possesses a mental dimension, or if it is not, in fact, so minuscule as not to merit consideration. As an impartial worshipper of the fair sex, I in no way advocate this position; for the sake of thoroughness, however, I cannot omit opinion relative to the matter; it is the following:

We usually consider woman from the wrong side altogether. What tends to receive notice in her is actually just the stuffed armature available to the essential part: *clothing*, which constitutes the true personality of the female. Doesn't a woman need a head along the lines that a hat needs one, or a wig a stand? Verily, we can see that the female head is admirably suited to keeping a bonnet or hat in the proper shape and fullness; that the brain basically serves no purpose other than to provide stuffing or padding to give the head the desired roundness so that what sits upon it will stay there; the faculty of understanding located inside plays the part of the soubrette in the fashion ensemble, busy day and night with selecting and fitting clothes, and, when called upon to do something else, protesting like a lady-in-waiting who has been asked to perform a task beneath her station (such as scrubbing the floor). Obviously, the joint at the neck serves no purpose other than to turn the bonnet, like meat on a skewer, toward anywhere there's a mirror, as if to cook its finery to perfection.—No woman would allow herself to be pinched and tortured by corsets and shoes, oppressed in altogether unhealthy manner, if her body weren't the most unimportant part of her, which must by right conform to the wishes of her lord and master, the dress. Indeed, there is nothing more probable than that the Creator, in order to compensate clothing, which is altogether secondary for a man, gave it woman as a slave, a kind of articulated doll, so it could make lovely folds and indulge its many moods freely; after all, dress alone determines whether a woman goes out for a stroll, attends church, or lets herself be seen in the first place. We need only observe females: what does the one notice and envy in the other besides the dress she's wearing? And should it ever occur to a man to find anything other than the attire of a lady worthy of attention, all the other women around will remark a lack of taste and, by devoting proportionally more care to their own clothing, direct him toward the truly vital parts of themselves. Even if she would not admit so openly, one woman credits another with real sense only when she sees her wearing an artful and cleverly put-together outfit; manifestly, then, insofar as she can be said to have one at all, the soul of woman lies in her clothes, and the rest of her is to be viewed as so much ossature for the dress, the true body and veritable flesh, to have a seat. Surely it is for this reason that prohibitions against exposed necks, bosoms, and arms have been taken comparable to measures against purely decorative columns in architecture (which are only supposed to hold up the ceiling); accordingly, so as not to violate the appointed order, women seek, when possible, a ring for each finger so each one of them will be carrying something. Were the dress originally and *a priori* shaped like a soap bubble, then the whole woman, without detriment to her inner nature, could be as round as a ball without protrusions and curves all over the place. Indeed, she would have to be—so as not to be considered bumpy and poorly suited to her destiny, a *monstrum per excessum*.

This theory, which takes only one aspect of woman into consideration, is undeniably very one-sided—as one-sided, in fact, as materialism and idealism are in philosophy, which also permit just one dimension of human being to count as valid. After all, the truth lies in-between. Just as mind and body possess equal dignity in man, so do body and attire in woman; for my own part, I affirm that the latter is the ideal and the former the real side of the female.

Having dealt with an opinion that leaves woman with nothing but a few good scraps, I can now step closer to completing the assigned task by touching on psychical qualities; although many more could be adduced, I would simply draw attention to one key point of difference; for the main, the classifications proposed by natural scientists concern physical characteristics; many admit that ways of creaturely life based on psychic operations do not fall within their purview.

I don't believe it takes much to recognize that the faculty of judgment does not guide woman so much as instinctual appetite; at very least, the former represents a small, stunted dwarf with whom the latter does not deign to exchange many words; according to all philosophers, however, the opposite is the case for human beings:

instinct amounts only to a nose, and one that smells quite poorly at that, by means of which the will and understanding sniff out game. On this score, the sage interpreters of Brahmanic law declare that the lusts of the female can be sated as little as fire with wood, the ocean deep with streams, or the kingdom of the dead with departed human beings and beasts. While these words are a little strong, I would advise any man who knows how perilous the instinctual longings of even the gentlest animal are not to stand in the way of his wife covetous of, say, a beautiful dress or scarf, even if she is as unable to articulate a sensible reason why she feels such immense desire for a red rag as a turkey cock might offer for his anger upon seeing the same.

Women's great love for children must also stem from such instincts, for if it were based on something other than what prevails among lower creatures, children would receive treatment more reasonable and beneficial to them. It is singular indeed how this love finds expression. Just as the latest scientific findings declare that the child in the womb must pass, from its germinal state until fully formed, through all the stages of animal life, so too does the female believe, once the child has entered the world, that nothing can demonstrate motherly love more than calling her offspring by names that rehearse the process all over again: *squirt*, *tadpole*, *mite*, *urchin*, *duckie*, *bunnikins*, *cub*, *pup*, and *little monkey*. Of course, when the child has reached this point of development, the father usually steps in to steer the course of growth up through the higher species: *louse*, *snake*, *minx*, *popinjay*, *jackass*, *baboon*, and the whole gamut of livestock. It may well be, since most freaks of nature come from a child getting stuck at a level of development which is supposed to be a transitory stage in the womb, that moral abnormalities occur when parents don't allow their young to complete the full cycle. The child halted at the primeval level of a worm by excessive maternal love presents a piteous sight, stopped up with a pacifier and bound in a swaddling straitjacket so it can be manipulated and mollycoddled for the mother's pleasure alone! It is generally held that little girls learn the ways they wrap, bind, and bend their dolls from the treatment administered to children brought by the stork; however, I maintain the contrary: that mothers transfer the treatment they found fitting for their playthings to the living dolls now in their clutches.

With that, we come to the main characteristics of the female constitution, which set the course for further discussion.

First and foremost, there's the long tail at the back of the head, the likes of which are not to be found in any other kind of animal, which would seem to have ascended to this height so that, with the enormous length it is known sometimes to reach and the lack of muscular fiber for keeping it straight, it will not drag in the dirt; this precaution strikes me as wholly unnecessary, incidentally, since women already twist together their caudal hairs into an artful braid and, by this means, prevent the same—which means, as I see it, that the tail could just as well have fit in its conventional place as in other animal species; but who can fathom the works of the Creator? At any rate, such appendages are often called "pigtail" or "ponytail."

Another feature to be mentioned here is the singular nature of tear ducts in women. In light of their output, one would assume them to be immense in size, and the lachrymal sac, appointed for holding the tears, at least as large as the bladder, which discharges a similar function elsewhere; however, the frequent evacuation of liquid makes such dimensions unnecessary. The tear ducts clearly serve an entirely different purpose in women than in men. Just as skunks, toads, and various other beasts will spray a moist substance to deter pursuers in the event of attack, women will secrete liquid in profusion when they are afraid, or sense danger, so predators will stay away. The strategy often proves successful, and kindly nature has given them the ability to increase or diminish, at will, the output of this vital stuff; with rare exceptions, the male lacks this faculty. On the occasion, I would venture a proposal sure to find welcome in lands without salt mines. As tears are known to contain a significant proportion of table salt, why not employ the ducts of women to obtain the same? More abundant and inexhaustible sources are hardly to be found, and it wouldn't be hard to make them even more productive. Simply stepping on the tail of a lapdog would yield enough to salt a stick of butter, and a missed evening on the town would do for a barrel of herring; an unfaithful beau would equip an entire household for a few years. The German expression, "to eat one's bread with tears," would cease to be figural and simply refer to putting some salt on it—as one often does, anyway. Before closing the book on the subject, I would implore all women concerned with maintaining their well-being to keep their tear ducts open and flowing, inasmuch as it is my heartfelt belief that constipation of the same will entail dropsy throughout the organism, which is readily explained by an excess of liquids. I would also alert young physicians to the matter; to date, they have paid too little attention to the cause for water retention, which occurs more frequently in the female sex than the male one.

And just as the greater development of the lachrymal organ sets woman apart from man, so too does she differ from him in the extraordinarily prominent function of the diaphragm and a virtuosic command of its musical properties, which the male never achieves. Without particular effort, and some twenty times a day, women perform the famous trick of the ancient magician who transformed a crying visage into a laughing one in an instant. If sudden changes of weather occur in the sky for no apparent reason, the same happens in the faces of women—a reflection of the heavens that repeats, in microcosm, events taking place in the macrocosm. All at once, a deluge pours down over a face clouded with trouble, only to give way to the sunny splendor of smiling cheer; then, before the observer can get his bearings, hail and storm winds thunder down, which no barometer could predict.

A phenomenon that has received no adequate explanation until now is that laughter exercises a beneficial influence on women's teeth. Without fail, one finds, the more a lady laughs, the prettier, whiter, and more regular her dentition will be. Women who never crack their mouths to smile usually have black teeth, or none at all. Accordingly, it's impossible to recommend strongly enough that women open up as often and as wide as they can to counter dental woes. The only exemption I would make is for those attended by young and inexperienced doctors, who might be induced to dangerous error inasmuch as medical textbooks declare involuntary laughter to betoken inflammation of the diaphragm or another sensitive organ; when no cause for laughter is in evidence, it's only too easy to diagnose an indisposition and prescribe the poor patient a regime of saltpeter and bloodletting, which will prove unavailing. Truly, there is no clumsier error than to think that women can laugh on such occasions as men tend to do, since usually the reason they laugh is simply that they don't feel like crying and are basically unable to keep their facial muscles in a state of rest for so much as an instant. Such muscular liveliness provides a further point of difference, and it is particularly noticeable in the female mouth. In keeping with the principle of natural philosophy that declares each inorganic thing to have an organic counterpart, it can be viewed as clockwork or a millwheel, since it rests as little as these devices do and likewise ceaselessly generates noise, making it impossible, when several such machines are grinding in concert, to hear one's own thoughts. As a rule, the verbiage generated by this constant motion of the mouth is of as little significance and import as only the creaking of a millwheel can be. And just as a lady is wont to go on a stroll to give her lapdog its requisite exercise, here the words just trot along so that the mouth will get the workout it needs. Surely a woman whose mouth were closed by force—admittedly, a contrivance for doing so has yet to be invented—would soon expire from cramps or epilepsy inasmuch as the local twitches of the mouth that have become necessary to female nature would spread system-wide to vent themselves, as it were. Incidentally, the process would offer a suitable means for many a cross-bearing husband to free himself from two afflictions at once: his spouse's talkativeness and his lady wife herself. This is also why a woman will feel well so long as her oral machinery is still going strong, and the logorrhea that occurs hereby is, in this regard, of vital importance. Should one notice that a woman has emitted no word for a quarter-hour, it may be concluded that she is either deaf and mute, at death's door, or not a woman at all; *quartum non datur*. Most regrettably, those who undertake to solve physical and mathematical problems no longer lend an ear to Nature, which has so often shown the way. It is said that humankind learned to build houses from the beaver, weaving from the spider, and seafaring from some other animal I can't remember at the moment. Surely Nature intended to provide man with the model of a *perpetuum mobile* in the female mouth, since, without power from water or wind, it is steadily in motion. At any rate, if such a thing exists, it is to be found here. Meanwhile, one might attempt to attach a simple machine for grinding or the like, so that the energy does not go unused and at least benefits the commonwealth a little.

I will now briefly summarize the remaining traits distinguishing woman from man so the final balance may be drawn. First, there's the smaller brain of the woman—a point that could also be made without anatomical investigation beforehand—which might in fact have been considerably smaller, were it not that that it coordinates so many nerves: those of the lachrymal organ, corners of the mouth, and even the hearing apparatus; women endeavor to bring the latter to the optimal state of operation by using keyholes and other apertures for eavesdropping.—Second, women lack a beard. We cannot praise the Creator highly enough for failing to provide one: were women to grow a beard, men would likely tear out their own in dismay. Women routinely require half a day to put the hair on their heads in order, which means that men are left in want of food. Would there be any time for housekeeping at all if grooming the female beard took away the other half? How, moreover, could a man provide for a wife already bankrupting him with her headdress, if now he had to finance the decoration of her chin? I can just picture the array of ribbons, pins, combs, and pearls the ingenious talent of the ladies would manage to find. Anyway, women cannot grow a beard for physical reasons: the motion of the lower jaw discussed above prevents the development of the same, just as constant agitation of a chemical solution keeps crystals from precipitating.—Third, this is the place to note the contrapuntal, treble voice of females, to which Leibniz might have pointed in his *Theodicy* as proof of overall teleological design: if the *allegro* and *presto* of women's song also governed the bass register, how would the infrequent and emphatic notes of the male instrument have room to resonate?

Contributing even a single word to conversation in the company of women, which now is possible only because the male voice is lower, would remain a bootless endeavor.—Fourth and last, I would draw attention to the delicate and fine skin of the female, which at some places, the cheeks, in particular, would seem a veritable mine for carmine and cinnabar, and on occasion traces of galena. Women's cheeks admit comparison with walls of niter inasmuch as, the older and more unremarkable they appear to be, the more the minerals mentioned above are produced under the surface, which one might collect with each new dawn in sizeable quantity.

What objection to the distinguishing features we have adduced could there possibly be? If it is already the case that a canine tooth prompts the zoologist, and a calyx the botanist, to feel justified in declaring a new species, why should we hesitate, for even a moment, to place women in a class separate from human beings? After all, they differ markedly in so many respects. Yet doing so raises a difficult question. What place in the overall scheme of things will women occupy, once set apart from the human race? In such a light, I believe, everyone will condescend to grant them the place of honor, hitherto occupied by the undeserving ape, right next to human beings. It is my hope that the female race will be gratified if I hereby restore it to its natural station.

FANTASIA, TO WOMEN

Everywhere, Force is but the staff on which Beauty leans so she can spread her blossoms without a care in the world, and though otherwise unyielding, the former is glad to bend his iron back, if only she will point the way with a gentle wand of lilies. Safely, Beauty toys with his hard, sharp weapon—the blade that gives way to nothing, yet melts at her touch. Force swells his angry muscles to break fetters that are imposed under duress, but when Beauty deploys her flowery bonds, he takes mincing steps to avoid breaking them. Just to offer Beauty a greater bridal gift, he would conquer the world; he strives to grow to the heavens to be able to take a deeper bow, so that he, the slave, may show himself worthy of her.

The Creator poured force into the limbs of man, placed the neck of the earth under his foot, and told it: "Serve him!" But He took the wings from the angel of beauty and gentleness so these qualities would remain down below and said: "Go to man and look upon him, that he may already glimpse heaven in your gaze." Man rose from his first slumber, and there stood woman, looking upon him. Not only did he glimpse heaven; he thought he had found it here.—Not man, but woman was the capstone, the crown, after which the earth could bring forth nothing lovelier and Creation ceased. The rocky cliffs adorned themselves with soft and bright tapestry; thorny bushes shot forth fragrant roses; the delicate vine twisted about the sturdy oak. Nature's fecund fantasy overflowed as her Symbols published the hour of woman's birth.

Nature had distributed all her gifts among her lesser children. There stood woman without defense, so the great mother wrapped the girdle of charm about her body and placed the dewdrop in her flowery eye: she needs no other weapons, for she commands magic.

Woman's sparkling glance has reduced cities and lands to ashes. A tiny tear can set swaths of the earth aflame or quench their fires. When she falls silent, a stream of eloquence more vital than a thousand thundering words from the likes of Cicero flows from the crimson waves of her tranquil lips. She utters a single syllable, and a proud, manly breast cannot contain the bliss it rouses.

"What is it, upon touching the mere hem of your dress, my nerves shudder, as with the surge of the tide? Why does nature, with all her gleaming jewels, lose her diamantine brilliance and simply set you into relief? Why do I lose sight of the infinite universe and see only you, the lustrous center around which I spin, a thirsting orb? Brightness appears only where your eye casts its beam. Why does my fancy, else the mind's untethered pinion, sit and brood before your image, flying back to its roost as soon as it takes wing? Why do I strike down the sacred images of my every ideal, just so I may kneel before your icon?—Isn't it because I have glimpsed heavenly heights in the loveliest of earthly temples? Is the butterfly of my imagination so restless because finally it has found the blossom it sought so blindly and impatiently, whose honeyed lips it would haunt forevermore? Does only now my own life shoot forth buds to intoxicate itself on the rapturous light peeking through the eyelid of a chalice yet unopened?"

Who would hazard the vain enterprise of depicting, with the flat colors of language, the flame that burns within? It's a youth whose broad chest a world entire would fill but halfway, whose untamed spirit casts off every rein; he has held fast to iron because his rough hand is fitted to nothing more delicate. A woman passed his way: the flower over which her foot glided did not tremble so much as flutter in delight, as toward a soft kiss. The coarse war chant in his breast became a sigh, and his weapon fell so his hand might catch the corsage that slid from her bosom. Before a god he would stand stiff-necked and proud, but willingly he bends knee and neck before her.

ON DEFINITIONS OF LIFE

Anyone who sets out to write a work of physiology looks first for a new definition of life. We have already had quite a few examples along these lines, and fortunately there's no need to learn how to go about living from the explanations offered in these books; everyone is born with an innate aptitude. Kant, from whose tree most of our newer philosophers (I leave exponents of natural philosophy aside) take the seeds for sprouting their own systems—and then, if but a few leaves happen to look different than the parent stock, inform the world that they have discovered an altogether new genus—Kant, I say, explains life as the capacity of a substance to determine its course of development on the basis of an inner principle. But what's an inner principle? If, as he seems to suggest, it is the soul *qua* power to think and will, then our whole body is a cadaver—unless we assume that the leg, the hand, and so on each possesses a part of the soul as an immanent principle. According to Kiefer the *glandula pinealis*, according to Meckel the *corpus callosum*, and according to others still the cerebral ventricles are animate beings; from this throne, as it were, the soul issues instructions to the rest of the corporeal world; the bones, as peasants, must bear the burden of sustaining the state, receiving scant recompense for their toil; the nerves, or nobility, give orders and bully the limbs as military officers arrayed in the red uniform of the muscle system; the veins represent the merchant class, circulating the *succus* and *sanguis* of life and trading goods at the borders, where each organ is charged with learning a trade; the head houses a whole university, with chairs for philosophy, mathematics, theosophy, and music; thieves lurk behind the ear, the occiput is home to libertines, and so on. Ultimately, only the queen bee—reason—is truly alive in this vast state; the rest is clockwork running from morning to night. If, in fact, what determines activity from the inside out is an inner principle, then it also inhabits the stone as *heaviness*: as such, when one rock presses on, or bumps against, another rock, it might not have any lifestyle to speak of—or manners, since it doesn't excuse itself—but it certainly exhibits life, inasmuch as it musters all the energy it can. A stone has learned nothing other than to exert itself in this way: we dance, and it bumps; we laugh, and it bumps; we write a poem, and it's still bumping away; bumping is an activity, after all. To be sure, the stone bumps because it has to, but if we posit that our own inner principle is a free one, then reason itself is the deadest thing that can possibly be, for it can only act (subjectively) on the basis of adequate and necessary grounds it has not posited itself. But all this amounts to drops in an ocean that has already been poured over the head of the venerable Kant—who's pretty washed up, anyway.

Indeed, Jacobi avers that nothing can be called living unless a mental representation causes its motions; but then how would a meadow planted with artificial, Italian flowers differ from a natural one, in which the flowers experience youth and old age? What's more, and as stated previously, it would follow that our heart and veins amount to so many dead pipes, and we might as well install lead ones, which would last longer.

For Erhard, the nature of life concerns the capacity of movement to provide utility through the thing that is moved. I gladly concede that what we call "living" has the capacity to move for its own use and benefit; but then one could equally well say that the nature of life involves the capacity to eat and drink; the living soul does not eat and drink, and it also doesn't move. So if we're speaking of motion only figuratively, we might as well say that the soul eats and drinks, since it works with representations drawn from the raw stuff of intuition, which it digests through the understanding; alternatively, one could say that life is the capacity to be at rest *or* be active, the capacity to perform or suffer action—to receive or give—by turns, to incorporate foreign elements, etc., etc. It almost seems that these concocters of definitions have been running around the mighty oak of life, in whose gigantic vessels courses the sap of the world, and simply grabbing a leaf, a bright blossom that happens to cast a smile their way, or—when nothing else is in reach—a piece of bark to put into their physiological herbarium (which only contains dried up specimens, anyway). Just as *Quercus robur* stands written on the label affixed to a tiny piece of the tree in their book, they append the name of *Tree of Life* to a little fragment. But neither a single leaf, nor one hundred leaves placed end to end, will ever constitute the whole.

Treviranus—who, incidentally, is mentioned *honoris causa* and will scarcely take umbrage if an obscure party presumes to touch on his dignity—confidently affirms, in his *Biologie* (from which I have taken the other definitions here) that "(physical) life is a condition that external factors bring forth and sustain, but in which, notwithstanding this chance quality, the consistency of phenomena prevails." An example may clarify this definition: *A given human being is sired with all the best intentions by his father, who desires children, but on account of the sickly constitution adhering to this person, each gust of cold air, each case of chilly feet, brings him into a state of disorder; in brief, any and all chance events in the outside world trouble the normal course of physiological phenomena; the party in question passes by a house by chance, and by chance a brick falls from it and by chance knocks in his skull; the chance effects of air and water after three days lead organic decay to set in; with ongoing changes in the weather, deterioration continues on a course more regular than the same individual's biological functions would have allowed under otherwise identical conditions.* I can't imagine a more striking example of the relationship between the living and dead states in one individual. For this man, life obviously began with the condition that the brick, a chance effect from the external world, brought about, which subsequent matters of chance maintained. In contrast, his conception, which we might also designate a chance effect from without, was unable to bring forth life on its own and merely produced a condition displaying extreme irregularity and susceptible to the effects of external factors; as such, it would qualify as an inert, or dead, state.—Of course, Treviranus didn't mean to say that at all, so I must have misunderstood every term he proposes. It's too bad that it's so easy to make mistakes with definitions, which are supposed to facilitate understanding. It's like an empty lantern suited to brightening the surroundings, but only if you put a light in first; this light is precisely what a definition is supposed to be.

Trying to collect and enumerate the various definitions of life would be an effort in vain; life is so rich in distinct phenomena that centuries aren't enough for bringing all of them together, even though so many have already been gathered. Moreover, it seems that definitions of life serve one purpose before all else: to justify the patent of nobility that self-serving human beings would grant themselves above all other creatures, such that what does not show a close relation to man belongs to the *plebs* of the dead; and people (of whom there are many in recent years, to be sure) who wish to introduce unrestricted equality and promulgate a constitution according to which the same, impartial law should govern the earth and who therefore, as right-thinking citizens of the world, would grant the humble rock, stepped on and made to bear burdens until now, the same right to life as plants and animals in thanks for its efforts on behalf of the whole—these people, just as soon as they make an appearance, are branded outlaws and rebels against the age-old, inherited order of things, and the young generation warned against their snares.

I have thought long and hard about life; thereby, and as is so often the case when pursuing profound reflection, I ultimately found that I was thinking about nothing, that life does not exist at all. All explanations I had heard up to this point boiled down to something that fit death just as well, if not better. A thought impossible to compass, not a source of light but a vast shadow without end, descended upon my soul; before me I saw the world lying open, an immeasurable tomb; there weren't even flowers growing on the grave where the corpse was lying, for they were dead and buried, too; nor was there anyone who might have planted them or watered them with his tears; tears were just drops of water, without meaning; each soul was mechanical clockwork in the casing of the body, and thoughts were automata that clicked away and sprang into action because they had to, not because they wanted to; love and friendship were lonesome flashes of electricity in the night; my eye, long blind, now recognized their spark as mere effects of conduction; the sun beamed its friendly countenance, but the earth did not recognize what it was doing; the sun didn't know it was smiling, either; the world was a specter aping life, sending icy shivers down the spine of the beholder; cosmic harmony faded into the dead swing of a pendulum surging and ebbing this way and that, while the storm of sentiment in the breast could be measured by cubit and span; they were the same vibrations that could be gauged elsewhere, just made to resonate here by a more finely tuned instrument. I took stock of the whole mechanism, which consisted of countless, interconnected levers; one end of a given lever was located within a socket formerly known by the name of some animate creature, and the other end reached into the external world; when the inner part twitched and put the outer part into a corresponding motion, I saw what once I had believed to be a free action. What a fool I'd been! Now I recognized how the inner lever was set in motion by an outer lever so it would move in this particular way, and not another; in turn, the motion of the outer lever was determined by yet another lever, and so on, *ad infinitum*. "How, now!" I exclaimed, "There must be One, moving all levers and yet moved by none. Where is *He*, who is living?" And lo, before me opened a path, and a column bearing the inscription: *Follow this way. Where it ends stands the House of the Living, whence all levers are worked.* I hastened forth, down the path, thinking at every step I was approaching the goal. And when I had traveled forever, I stood again before the first column and recognized, there, the Symbol of the Circle.

THE GREATEST ARTIST

Our earth is an Aeolian harp into which God breathes the soul; its harmony does not sound forth in isolated notes, however; whole arts emerge in unison: each realm of colors, shapes, tones, and fragrances corresponds to a separate string stretched over the planet, struck together to bring forth One Chord. God plays the whole world as a single harmony in space, one great melody in time—or, more precisely, thousands of melodies, each of them complete in itself, are united by the mystery of His unfathomable counterpoint into the stream of One Harmony; the spirit flowing through the music in wondrous ways is fortune itself. Earth- and sun-systems perform the boundless dance of the spheres to this great symphony; their round takes the shape of resonant constellations in the cosmic concert, which has played since the first day of Creation. Dissonance, in myriad forms, rings forth from sinking worlds, the weeping and gnashing of teeth among peoples undone, jeering vice and persecuted virtue—for what would music be without dissonance?—but it all is resolved into consonance audible to the Author of the Great Work; for we hear only the resonant vibration of single atoms of His instruments; the rest passes over us in a rush. The mysterious triad winds its way throughout the whole of nature; the keys, as if each one were but a single note, harmoniously weave together into an organic, chiming system; each tone that joins with others is a harmony played on an instrument of its own; and each chord feels in itself what it expresses, and expresses only what it feels; for God's notes are alive, and being alive means nothing so much as reverberating into time as a sound struck on His harp.

All of God's music has but One Theme, the simplest one of all, resounding in every possible variation and performed in myriad ways, which never will finish until the end of the world. It would truly be terrible were God to strike the final note, and with its dying echo, the world dissolved into nothing and the pulses of life, which are simply a dance following the great harmony, ceased, if the intermittent pauses—night, or winter, when only half the strings sound, while the others rest—congealed into silence and the mighty instrument intoned its own swansong. But the Lord will never stop playing: His soul *is* harmony, harmony immortal and eternal. For God has no one with whom He might speak; outside Him is nothing; harp—the world—in hand, He speaks with Himself in sublime isolation, and thus does time run its course; luminous globes and dewy pearls roll forth as He plucks the strings: storms shaking the oceans of worlds, and within them buzzing bees, babbling brooks, and piping shepherds; all things that are shoot out as notes from His hand, and the *fortissimo* threatening to burst the seams of the world He has made the dusky background for placid and soothing tones.

All nature is God's portrait: He paints and He paints, and by painting ensures that the great likeness of Himself contains the smaller one; only the features become less apparent as the picture unfolds; thus, each crystal, flower, and plant, the vegetable kingdom and the whole organic world, each sun, array of planets, and the organic continuity between thousands of solar systems are His own image and tell of Him. With wondrous ease, the Lord sets down the features of His work, painting in just one stroke a thousand meadows and woods and in another stroke the variegated bloom of spring; a blink of the eye is all it takes to distribute light and shadow over an infinite landscape, where each thing emerges after its kind; when, as night falls, He obscures or covers up the painting, this occurs only so that it may be conjured up, more beautiful than ever, the following morning. The infinite canvas onto which God pours His colors is boundless space; His brush, never resting, brings forth ever-renewed time; masses of matter are His pigments, the world of forms the lines, and living creatures the figures painted. God sets down nothing in dead hues; each bright point is a complete work of art, comprising others, smaller than itself, and itself an element of another painting greater in size. The earth He has painted in myriad greens, a copious floral gown, is not worked from inert stuff but from living plants; each of the planets glows with its own blush, illuminated by a star assigned to it; the billions of heavenly bodies traversed by milky ways He has fashioned into a still-larger panorama; the points of shadow He adds are worlds veiled in night. Each of the paintings, big or small, God lays down as a sketch; then He fills out their finer forms, or has His pupils do so. God does not compose bit by bit, placing one part next to the other, joining leaf and flower to the stem already there. No, He sets down the Idea all at once, as a seed, and tells the sun: "Take up your brush of light and color and continue." Everywhere the Idea is His own. The execution is left to the artist, who is also created by God, so the work is elaborated in keeping with divine conception.

God has sought to depict the battle between Heaven and Hell in his cosmic canvas; thus, He took an expanse of infinite gloom as the backdrop and gazed upon it with an eye that does not receive, as ours does, but *gives*: the luminous thought of His fancy beamed into the night, and the sea of light split from the sea of darkness; lo, the first draft creating order: the surf of light and shade rear up and collide, breaking into myriad waves of brightness and obscurity that, as they crash together, take the form of virtue, beauty, truth, love, and salvation, held apart by, and occasionally struggling against, floods of darkness—vice, falsehood, hatred, and despair—before becoming reconciled and bringing forth color, the Symbol of surging, restless life.

God does not think *of* earths, suns, flowers, and His living creatures endowed with reason; He *thinks* earths, suns, flowers, and indeed us, ourselves, with all our reason. If a self-sufficient thought exists for us, then the thoughts that emerge alongside it, whatever they might concern, must also be real, for they are nothing less than what it *is*; they affect it and it affects them, each one reciprocally and in turn, and the faculty of reason, which thinks all thoughts, is the god of individual notions and regarded by them as their creator. Likewise, we are simply the particular thoughts in the great brain of God, and we call God's mental images of plants, beasts, and stars real things because we, who call ourselves real too, exist in their company and at their side; time is the course of God's thoughts, space the delineation of His fantasy, and the cause-and-effect of the material world connections between His ideas. A tree sprouting from a seed is a system He unfolds out of a principle, adding some qualities and subtracting others. By the same logic, God has brought forth and combined all His thoughts; the same mental law—which we call the Law of Nature—prevails in each cycle and stage, exercising dominion over matter in all its forms. And this God, for whom we are mere thoughts, is Himself but a thought of Himself, of God-greater-still.

God is the greatest, the sole, poet; His work is Creation, an overwhelming drama of which a thousand years of history represent but a fragment; nations are its protagonists, speaking to each other like individual human beings on the stage, offering a hand as a token of amity or giving in to simmering rage that erupts in violence. What poet can match the objectivity of the Lord? In the song He sings, the storm thunders, the cascade rushes down mountain passes, and we see the idyllic sport of shepherd and shepherdess—all of it has issued from His innermost sentiment. God's poem comprises infinite verses, not strung end to end, but intoned with lyrical ardor and lyrical cadence; the second stanza develops the idea of the preceding; and now, in the third, when He has led the poem through myriad flowering likenesses and images, He takes hold of these likenesses and images again, reworking each according to the first, general Idea, and thus the unified theme unfolds, ever more radiant and majestic than before. God lets the characters He introduces in His poems, His dramas, act and contend against each other, from the beginning to the end of their time onstage, according to the idea in which He first conceived them, so that each one develops uniquely in its thousandfold variation. His drama does not join one episode lifelessly to the other; new branches shoot forth, which could not have grown without the rootstock of burgeoning life within. Each scene is complete unto itself but forms part of a greater play: one knot is untied, but only so the thread may be taken up and woven, with others, into a new one. The world is one vast tragedy, which began with God's birth. He is the only hero in His drama, and it will end with His death. Yet He was born before time, and He will die at the end of infinity—that is to say, never.

Art, our own, does not imitate the works of the Great Master presiding over nature, but it ought to copy its spirit. All the rules of our art are Laws of Nature.

THE WORLD UPSIDE DOWN

One can hardly arrive at notions more nonsensical in appearance than by picturing the whole world as clockwork running backward in space and time, so that, at all points, *consequence* becomes *antecedence*, and vice versa. In such a world, one goes to sleep when most awake and rises rubbing one's eyes in exhaustion. Birth is a matter of worms and plants emitting substances from which a shrunken old man is congealed who, as the years pass by, grows younger and younger, finally becoming a child: the most venerable sage winds up screaming in diapers and ends his life by entering the body of a woman and dissolving into its vital substance. Blows to the head, poisons, and the like act as invigorating forces, for one always feels better afterward. Cemeteries are places where people are born, and midwives ply their trade at tombs; the act of procreation is death itself, which ushers human being into the void. Conversations unfold in such a way that one knows what one has said only after having spoken; scenes of reconciliation herald incipient quarrel; punishment precedes the crime, and reward the virtuous deed, since both occur after the fact; the murderer who loses his head must stand and prove his execution justified. People are dirtiest after they have bathed, and beards are unshaved onto the face. Many a craftsman receives emolument years before making a pair of boots or a coat; indeed, it may happen that a garment is paid for, but never supplied by the tailor. People start eating at their fullest and look up from their plates in hunger; at the same time, and to the contrary, eating does not occur *a priori* so much as *a posteriori*, with manure from the field entering the human body and there being processed into meat, apples, potatoes, and assorted vegetables that exit through the mouth; fruit falls up into the trees and turns into a flower, which then becomes a bud; ultimately, the tree shrinks into a seed; meat passes into the pot in order to be cooked until it's raw; on the butcher's block it compounds itself into a solid mass yielding oxen, sheep, and so forth. The man who manages to acquire a torn coat or a ramshackle house considers himself lucky; the newer things look, the closer they stand to annihilation; garments, cut into rags by the clothier, make their way to the fabric store, and from there to the textile plant, and on to the wool wholesaler; all these people labor to prepare attire for an animal, duly cut into place by the sheepshearer; everywhere human beings look like the servants of beasts; instead of being despoiled by the former, animals make everything human their own.

How would it be, were such a sentence passed—if the world, after running forward for a spell, started going the other way? It would be no different than what is the case now, with God progressively transforming Himself into the world—the general taking form as the particular—except that the world, headed in reverse, would turn into God: human beings would become their first parents, from whom they once issued, until all that is left is the great, absolute Nothing posited by natural philosophy. But a world such as this is nothing impossible, for if the universal law is turned on its head, the relationship between elements continues to hold; an infinite series may be read in one direction or the other, if only by the lights of an infinite Being; either way it obeys One Principle. Any word that can be uttered can also be spoken backward.

IDEA FOR A HIGHER CULINARY ART

To date, cuisine has more or less stood first and foremost among the arts *in praxis*; yet behind its back (that is, when not at the table), wagging tongues have often belittled it and denied it the laurels it is due. Hereby, it may be that the culinary art will be ennobled and counted among higher pursuits—just as the player's art formerly qualified as dishonest, so long as it was nothing but crude pratfalls represented on festive evenings, but now an actor can be held in higher regard than the hero he portrays; the only question is whether, by nature, cuisine admits such refinement.

If, in essence, all fine art seeks to evoke the better sort of thought, feeling, and endeavor by lending sensory form to, and expressing, higher mental faculties, then cuisine, insofar as it aims merely to satisfy the palate, cannot pretend to this title; just as little would painting merit being called a fine art, if it contented itself with trying to entertain the eye through contrasts between, and combinations of, colors without relation to a determinate idea; the same would hold for music, if it just threw together notes like so much gibberish for the ear, but supplied no intellectual feeling. But if the culinary art should prove able to rouse higher, mental activity by giving it shape and sense, no exception is to be taken to placing it in such illustrious company.

A certain material lies at the ready for each of the arts: painting has colors, music has notes, and architecture employs stones, wood, and so on. Form consists of combinations of, or connections between, substances; in painting, it's how pigments blend into each other and stand apart; in music, the variation of tones yield rhythm, harmony, and melody; in architecture it's a matter of how rocks and lumber are assembled. In turn, a distinction is made between inner and outer form; the latter concerns the way materials are put together and presented to the sensory apparatus; for example, poetry marshals words, metrical feet, rhyme, and so on; music enlists various instruments playing in concert, and so on. Inner form concerns the effect on sentiment and the mind (about which we will have more to say in a moment); with poetry, it's the way the thoughts underlying the verbal work of art fit together in terms of the overall design; with music, it's the spirit animating harmony, melody, and so forth.

The art of cooking has at its disposal all the substances that can be taken in and assimilated by the human organism; its form consists of the manner in which substances are put together: their visible arrangement and their chemical composition. The underlying idea, as elaborated to date, is to achieve the most pleasing flavor possible, that is, *Beauty* insofar as it connects with the sense of taste. In this regard, the culinary art can have no greater temple than the kitchen; in my opinion, however, still more is possible, and Cinderella may be promoted to the status of muse. Here, a bit more detail is in order.

Basically, we are equipped with two inner senses. The first is mental and apprises us of the state of our soul; in a mirror, as it were, we glimpse sad and happy conditions: hopes and fears, hatreds and loves, heartening and doubtful moods, and so on. This sense, known simply as "inner feeling," gives us self-awareness in the first place and can scarcely be separated from it; it is where all the impressions made by art, and absorbed from outside, pool together; sight, hearing, smell, taste, and sensation are so many strings, plucked by one art or another; inner feeling is the chamber where they resonate.

The other sense, which can also be called an inner feeling, has come to be known as general physiological sensibility; it reports to us, as our psychological sensibility registers our mind's activities, the conditions and processes at work in the body; admittedly, these impressions are relayed inwardly, such that our own organic life seems to be external to the soul itself. This inward corporeal sensibility includes feelings of pain and contentment, whether general or localized, hunger and thirst, fatigue and vigor, tingles, twitches, and itching, warmth and cold—in brief, all modifications to which our bodies are subject.

Since it's impossible to picture the relationship between the various levels of sensibility in anything but schematic terms, I will provide one general model: the universal scheme affording a picture of the connections within each and every organism, as well as those of the particular spheres constituting it.

Imagine a circle. The inner psychic sense that apprehends mental phenomena can be thought to occupy the center; only in relation to it do all the other senses come to possess their own, independent reality; the periphery, which borders the external world, represents the physical senses through which all impressions from without must pass to reach the interior; the radii between the center and the periphery are our general physiological sensibility; from here, not only sensations from outside are transmitted; because whatever is seen, heard, and so on is initially registered as a modification of our own body, our immediate corporeal feelings of selfhood are, as well. Picturing this circle as organically integrated with the rest of our being, we see how our physiological sensibility merges with the outer senses while still claiming a sphere of its own.

To date, all the fine arts have been conceived either as enlisting an outer sense to provoke inner feeling, as occurs in painting, music, dance, and so on; or as affecting the soul directly, that is, transmitting the psychic movements that are supposed to touch inner feeling without making use of another sense—as is the case with poetry, which does not act by way of sight, hearing, or touch so much as through a verbal substance that, while received from without, is grasped by the soul alone and is neither a matter of how words are composed nor of how phrases are arranged; in terms of conception, pure gibberish could be a poem, if only a fitting language were devised—a rule that applies neither to music nor to painting. To employ an admittedly indefinite comparison: poetry is the spiritual reflection of all the other arts. But even so, it seems we lack an art that touches our inner sense by harmoniously stimulating the physiological sensibility; such an art, I submit, is what cooking—if the name is to be retained—might become, provided its throne is no longer the tongue, but the whole of embodied, human being. Its elements can no longer be meat, bread, cabbage, and the like, the stuff of everyday life corresponding to the unpoetic and unmusical language of day-to-day activity; like true music, the higher culinary art requires instruments and intervals endowed with a deeper meaning.

If I seek to rouse or heighten cheer in someone by means of art, I will play a musical composition that displays this quality, arrange for a happy dance to be performed, or take him to a garden that expresses joyful life; I can also endeavor to bestir his inner feeling by means of a cheerful poem or song. However, our culinary art has already arrived at a point that I may seek to induce cheerfulness by way of physiological sentiment, offering, say, a cup of good coffee or a glass of wine. In all these cases, it is not a matter of the substance itself awakening a cheerful feeling; it is not the notes themselves, not the words or gestures, that induce a good mood, for another arrangement of the same would bring about the opposite; rather, how they are connected underlies the sense of happiness—or, put a little differently, it is the form into which the material has been brought that achieves this particular effect.

Likewise, with coffee and wine, it is not the substance in itself that finds expression in our body and mind; like all vegetable matter, coffee and wine consist of hydrogen, carbon, oxygen, and a little nitrogen; on their own, these components are indifferent in nature or express themselves in only the broadest terms; the reason for their effect on our organism derives from the inner (chemical) form of these combined elements, the way they are mixed together.

The examples provided, coffee and wine, are substances that did not come about by artificial composition; they are sprung from the hands of nature; therefore, if they have an effect on us, this occurs along the same lines that we are moved by her great works of art: lovely landscapes, stormy skies, and so on; they are not fitted to a purpose by human hands; instead, their artful influence is already founded in their natural composition. Yet the effects to be achieved by such substances can only flourish and become more pronounced when knowingly shaped by the artistic hand of man.

Indeed, there is scarcely a physical sensation—or, for that matter, a mental one—that cannot be roused by means of a material substance. Even if Hahnemann's *Arzneimittellehre* exaggerates the effects of various medicinal compounds on our bodies, enough of what the book says is true, and proven by experience, to secure the basis of our new art.

A few examples are in order.

If I take just one color to paint something, I can provide the most general outline, but most of the figure to be depicted remains undefined, as is the case with silhouettes, which use only black; however, as soon as I can add another color—for instance, put white on black—it is possible to execute the whole figure with utmost precision, heightened by every additional color employed, provided, of course, that they are not thrown together arbitrarily.—Say I wish to draw a triangle, with lengths already given for the base and one side; using the measurement of the side as a radius, I draw a half-circle from one of the end points of the base to obtain a midpoint; I know that the half-circle includes the geometrical location of the top of the triangle, but the latter still could occupy any point along this continuum; in order to find the exact spot I now draw, with a third line as radius, a circle from the other end of the base: where both circles intersect, the vertex stands.—Gold displays a range of qualities, and so does a sphere; gold can assume an infinite number of shapes, and a sphere can be made from an infinite number of materials; but if one speaks of a golden sphere, there is hardly room to add anything more, since the two terms define each other.

A similar principle applies elsewhere; not much can be done with a monochord instrument, but with two, three, or more strings it is possible to approach a full realization of sonorous potential and bring forth musical works of art with greater definition; one note either has no character at all or it has universal character, since it can be paired with any other note.—The rule holds: the more that things expressing general effects on their own are combined and integrated with each other, the more particular the result will be.

Thus, if I drink only coffee, it's true that the beverage—provided it's well made and one is not the sort who drinks it day in and day out—will induce cheer and a sense of lightness; this effect remains general and much about it is still undefined: the exhilaration can find expression in one set of ideas or an entirely different one, and the feeling of ease may act upon one organ more than another; consequently, it does not qualify as a matter of art; however, if I consume another substance along with the coffee, right after drinking it, or add it to the coffee itself—a substance that also elicits general effects, but different ones—then, through such a combination, an infinitely more specific effect will be brought forth: the elevated mood will become more determinate in one particular way or another; different combinations, sensibly guided, of course, will make the effect even more specific and in this way achieve any number of artful effects. By the same token, combining many lines enables one to construct and draw any figure, multiple colors will reproduce whatever strikes the eye, the arrangement of many notes brings forth music to rouse varied sentiments, and connecting several characteristics yields anything that can be conceived, and so forth.

But take an instrument with just three strings, which already allows pleasant pieces to be played; if one tells someone who knows nothing of the relationship between notes, and has no intuitive sense of them at all, that it will bring forth splendid music, he will take it in hand and bring forth a miserable racket, then snort in derision at whoever claims that the instrument produces harmony.—Give paint and brushes to someone who does not understand how to combine colors or draw properly and tell him that he has the means not only to imitate the variegated majesty of nature, but to surpass it; he will discolor the paper and marvel that you were foolish enough to imagine fine art can be made in this way.—Give a man a bar of sulfur, bottled oxygen, a few pieces of quicklime, and tell him he can make plaster from it. If he doesn't know the basics of chemistry, he'll grind up the sulfur and lime in proportions dictated by chance, then dump them into the bottle, whereby the greater part of the oxygen will escape—the analogy isn't far to seek—and to his astonishment, he'll find he has some batch of sulfur, lime, and oxygen but no plaster; and yet, these same substances do combine into plaster, provided one mixes the right amounts together under proper conditions.

With regard to what we know about how various substances affect the body, we are still at the same level as the person described above—one simply handed an instrument, brush and paints, or chemical elements. At best we can see what each substance does, or hear how each note sounds on its own; we are incapable of achieving a harmonious combination in the right proportions and following the proper order; someone who smears together colors to produce the illusion of marble or strikes piano keys at random is more or less acting as sensibly as a pharmacist compounding drugs according to a formula; but the results are not much to speak of.—Therefore, the fact that nothing to date has been achieved in our art should not lead one to believe that nothing will ever be accomplished. At very least, there are hints of what may yet come to pass.

We already know the capacity of many substances to induce quite pleasant effects, some of them physical and others mental, on the basis of their composition; examples include opium, coffee, wine, or a dose of fresh air; we also know about those with disagreeable effects; instead of well-being and heightened vitality, they provoke nausea, pain, melancholy, and so on. With the infinite multiplicity of substances, we possess a rich store, if I may recur once again to metaphorical language, for bringing forth varied transitions from one state of harmony to another, duly rousing discordance (a feeling of pain) so that it may resolve, with the proper antidote, into counterpoint, stimulating first one, then another part of human life—or, to be more precise, the whole of human being from one side, then another—just as a piece of music, which has a more limited scope, acts upon our sensibility in different ways. As yet, we can scarcely know what substances, and in what combinations, may be employed to particular ends, but narcotics will be preferred for obtaining a direct effect on the psyche. The properties of opium in this regard are established. Thus, one reads in Keil's *Fieberlehre*: "Superstitious people are said to make suppositories from the seed of the thorn apple, or to daub their foreheads with the oil of the same, which places them in a state whereby they imagine themselves to be in contact with spirits and devils. The same effects are produced by the leaves and roots. According to Kämpfer," he continues, "the Brahmins of Malabar have a paste compounded from the seeds of the thorn apple, poppy juice, and hemp pollen; by this means, they effect the strangest confusion of human understanding, from which they profit in religious ceremonies to deceive the people. Kämpfer and his friends ingested a little bit of the substance, found themselves extraordinarily exhilarated and started laughing violently; when, toward nightfall, they rode back home on horseback, they thought they were coursing through the clouds, surrounded by a rainbow."

Orfila writes: "If the leaf of *Datura ferox*, which grows wild in the warmer parts of China and East India, is applied to the edge of a glass, anyone drinking from it and placing his lips on the affected part is said to succumb to a brief spell of rage." Needless to say, strong effects of this kind can be mitigated at will.

It is also known that, in earlier times, ointment made from mandrake root (*Atropa mandragora*) was employed to stimulate all manner of visions, prompting one to believe in commerce with spirits and devils.

In addition, this category of substance includes *Cicuta*, *Belladonna*, *Hyosciamus*, tobacco by its very nature, all other kinds of *Datura*, and countless plants, all of which act powerfully on the same part of the human organism—or, at any rate, largely overlap in their influence, even if each one produces specific results, which have also been recorded. Inasmuch as using one of these many substances occasions general and indeterminate effects on the mind, it seems plausible that combined application of the same in the proper form and proportion, and with correct preparation, would bring about quite certain and well-defined movements of disposition and mood; a compound designed to induce a certain state of mind might just as rightly be called a work of art as a musical composition, which also has an effect only through the arrangement of notes that, in themselves, are insignificant; here, too, analogies to harmony and melody will be readily found; substances acting simultaneously correspond to the former in the new culinary art, since—as occurs in music—the concurrence of parts in agreement elicits a unified feeling; in turn, the order in which substances are consumed determines the flow of sentiment, corresponding to the role played by melody. (To be sure, developing the melody properly will be a matter of researching how long it takes for each component to produce its particular effect.)

If, then, one wishes to make a rough sketch of how a culinary work of art would be enjoyed, picture a person in an ideal state of health (for where disharmony prevails in the body, substances will produce a different effect), whom one has fast for one day—a necessary step, partly to enhance receptivity, and partly to prevent unanticipated side-effects from foodstuffs; this party is then given a menu, the equivalent of a sheet of music, outlining a culinary work that a celebrated artist (say, from the third or fourth millennium of the Common Era) has composed; here, as on the program for a drama, the "actors" and "roles" are written, or, as for a piece of music, the keys, modes, and instrumentation: the contents of vials and tins required for the production, as well as the time of day, temperature, and external conditions that will enhance the work or undermine its effectiveness. Just as a piece of music is often preceded by an indication of its intended effect or prefaced by a remark that it has been composed for a specific occasion—there are funeral and victory marches, songs of celebration and songs of war, and so forth—the culinary score might include mention, *To be consumed when sad*, *Description of a warrior's sentiment in battle*, *Piece for a leg*, *breast*, etc.—One would take first one glass, then another, in the rhythm prescribed by the meal's composer, who had arranged them in keeping with each component's capacity to induce transition from one effect to another or in light of their combined qualities; thus, seven drops from one vial and three from another would roll over the tongue, followed by a teaspoon of powder; one might chew a certain leaf, sniff at a flask, and so on and so forth, until one had eaten one's way through the piece; the finale would come from a substance that brought together the effects of all the others in a chorus of wholesome sentiment. Since, as a rule, a given substance's properties are felt only after some time has elapsed, our concertgoer would be sure to avoid noisome influences before the piece began to play in his organism and have found a quiet spot to sit down and give himself over to the sensations roused.

In this manner, one's very organism would become an instrument that makes and experiences music simultaneously; the substances are just the fingers with which it is played. Of course, the human organism is in fact a whole orchestra of varied instruments fitted with the subtlest strings, and each one demands to be played in a particular way if they are all to act in concert. As things stand today, alas, our culinary art of medicine tries to fiddle on the flute, and when wind instruments are in fashion, to blow upon the violin.

On this score, we must address one objection that might be made to the viability of producing such inner harmony.

Every human being has a particular physical constitution. It would seem, then, that substances will work in different ways on different people, such that no general rules can hold. There's no denying this fact, but since the effect of our culinary artworks will not depend on substances taken in isolation so much as the harmonious combination of several substances into a whole, a concordant result, determinate in nature, will find expression in each uniquely constituted human being while also displaying a general quality; in like manner, a piece of music will evoke one particular mood or setting more than another for a listener, without the overall effect of harmony going missing.

To be sure, one might ask: if, for thousands of years now, activity in apothecaries—with which our culinary art entertains a closer relation than it does with kitchens—has brought forth nothing that so much as hints at what is being proposed here, are we to expect that the means will be found to perfect this exalted pursuit?—Fortunately, such doubt is unwarranted. Compare the discoveries in physics and chemistry, made over the course of millennia, in relation to what the last fifty years have witnessed, and the gulf that stands between them. The seed of a science may slumber in the dust for ages before a ray of light descends and prompts it to shoot forth its radiant blossoms. I recall having read an apt analogy in one of Kiefer's works. Consider a blade of grass; the undermost nodes are spaced at quite some distance from one another; the plant has had to grow for some time before the lowest part gave way to the succeeding stage; yet the closer it comes to the top, the smaller the gap between nodes; in like manner do epochs notable for invention flow along: at the beginning, a long—often exhausting—period must pass, then discoveries succeed each other at increasingly rapid intervals, as science progresses toward full flower. One should not think, then, that if it has taken a science or art a thousand years to make one advance, only one more will be recorded in the next thousand. Indeed, it may rush forward by three, then five steps. If only in theory, I would conclude that progress follows such a course in general; the reasons for which now follow.

When a body falls from a state of rest, in the first second of free and unobstructed motion it covers about fifteen feet; but it would be mistaken to infer that it travels just fifteen feet more over the next second; no, it goes three times as far, that is, forty-five feet; in the third second of its fall, the distance is five times as great, or seventy-five feet, and so on for the rest of its course. In sum, then, it has traveled one times fifteen feet after the first second; one times fifteen plus three times fifteen after the following second, for a total of four times fifteen feet; after the third second, nine times fifteen; after the fourth, sixteen times fifteen, and so on and so forth, with the distance that is covered progressing by the squared value of the time it has been falling. Two forces are to be considered in this process: gravity, which would draw the body toward the earth in constant fashion, if it alone were active, and inertia, which would make the body continue to move from one second to the next at the speed it has already attained, were it not for the force of gravity. The combined effect of these two forces produces acceleration. Well, where cultural progress is concerned, the action of two equally marked forces is at work, which likewise determines acceleration, and with the same result. That is, humankind's general striving to arrive at greater perfection corresponds to the pull exercised by the earth's core, and the effect of inertia finds expression in the fact that each advance made toward fundamental knowledge facilitates the next step; the consequences of each step contribute to all advances that follow, just as inertia does when an object falls; the speed attained in a given interval represents the premise, as it were, for the velocities reached in all the temporal intervals to follow.—Strictly speaking, this law is subject to modification where longer spans of time are concerned, for gravity increases in inverse proportion to the square value of distances: the closer a body comes to the center of the earth, the more it is attracted by it; similarly, striving to attain the goal of science increases as proximity does. We can disregard changes in gravity and cultural ambition only when brief periods stand at issue; otherwise, the formula of acceleration applies here as much as there. But just as, strictly speaking, the calculated speed of a falling object exists only in theory—in actual fact, the resistance of air, winds, the earth's rotation, and other factors all modify motion—it would be foolish to expect the absolutely regular advance of culture at fixed intervals; given that fall time represents an item of fundamental importance, I believe that calculations such as those indicated above, while subject to correction, are not to be disregarded, even if they do not immediately appear to offer a practical use—which could only be attained if the mathematical approach taken here were extended to all branches of human life and endeavor; only then would it be possible to make the necessary adjustments, just as it is impossible to add corrections to the distance of a fall before calculating, with just as much mathematical precision, the value of the air resistance at work. (On its own, such computation is unavailing.)

I have made this digression en route to the main point; in essence, I just want to affirm that there is no call to despair about the viability of our culinary art just because so little has been done for it to date.

Indeed, one can already foresee how, one day, the project might achieve realization. A strictly empirical approach will not do, even though experimentation will necessarily play a role and, properly incorporated, make a vital contribution. In this regard, we cannot commend highly enough the method pioneered by Hahnemann, that is, the unblinkered study of effects produced by substances on a healthy organism without trying to group specific influences on various parts of the body in terms of general categories. At this point in time, in my view, doing so would be premature; at any rate, it would pose the same difficulty as setting out to classify a whole realm of Nature. Once the stoichiometric ratios between substances, their manifold relations to each other, have been explained—for instance, the crystalline form of the bodies they yield—the basis for a theory of culinary art and the application of the same will likely be found; Kiefer has already offered thoughts in this regard. When correct knowledge is obtained concerning the basic elements, and the proper figures established, it will be possible to replace a whole laboratory full of pots and pans with a single table of calculations and to determine the law governing proportions. By the same token, one will analyze the human body stoichiometrically; in light of its composition—once the main principle is found—theoretical reflection will readily identify relationships between substances and our organism. Incidentally, the stoichiometry must be different for organic bodies and inorganic ones. The first step would involve breaking down the body into organic parts—to which end nothing more sophisticated than the (admittedly crude) anatomist's scalpel has been found to date; in turn, these parts would be broken down progressively to the most basic organic elements—oxygen, hydrogen, carbon, nitrogen, and so on. The initial task would be to determine the relative role of the vascular, nervous, and cellular systems for a given organ; then, further analysis of the latter's constitution would be necessary. For the time being, all the physiological groundwork is missing, but even so, the undertaking is just as feasible as anything else is.

ON SCHEMATISM, OR SYMBOLS

It is a vain undertaking to speak of non-sensory things by means of other than sensory images: schemata, or symbols. All the relations that exist between our mental powers, all effects of, and relationships between, forces in general admit expression only to the extent that we lend them a physical husk; indeed, not only is it impossible to express them otherwise; they cannot be thought in the first place. Should I wish to share a concept, a rational idea, that has occurred to me, is there any way to express its connection to my thinking except to say that I had it "in mind"? Does this statement not rest on the formal representation of a vessel that is holding something? The psyche is pictured, however imprecisely, as a spatial schema into which an idea has been put. At the same time, when we think of something, the object is supposed to lie "outside" the mind; but since the mind is not a physical entity occupying space, the expression—whatever turn one gives it, it implies a spatial representation—is completely unsuited to mental events. Yet how else can the connection between the objects of thought and our mind be expressed? If we examine the nature and scope of our concepts, it's clear that logic as a whole is full of schemata like this, which impose themselves by way of the language we use, or occur in the visual form of so many circles; there's no question that anyone who wishes to grasp the content and scope of what is presented by logic must recur to such schematism, if only mentally. If, considering our intellectual operations, one thinks of the senses as taking in material for mental representations and our faculty of understanding as sifting it, splitting it apart, putting it together, and so on, what does one have for all these non-sensory actions but images borrowed from the realm of the senses? The images do not simply adhere to words; they are necessarily thought along with them whenever it's a matter of conceiving the relations between, and activities of, mental operations; and if one goes looking for other expressions, these remarks apply to them in equal measure. In point of fact, it is impossible to elucidate the nature of something non-sensory without symbols, and every relationship between non-sensory matters and anything else that has ever been elucidated owes its status to representation-in-a-symbol.

Take any philosophical system that presumes to represent non-sensory reality directly and examine it piece by piece. Just see whether it is not, at every point, schemata that are offered. Inner and outer processes, matter and form, subjective and objective phenomena, realms of light and obscurity all amount to efforts to name abstract, non-sensory things that, thanks to the power of the symbol expressed in the word, afford an intuitive understanding; meanwhile, other terms that do not display a schematic or symbolic aspect—understanding, reason, cause, effect, beauty, virtue, and so on—enter our consciousness only inasmuch as we think of them in terms of the senses, as schemata: we must imagine something physical acting as a cause, producing an effect, embodying beauty or virtue (for instance), or else come up with associations that ultimately prove to be schemata, too. Ordinary philosophy proceeds rather strangely on this score: it has found a certain set of schemata or symbols at the ready, or itself authorized them; and with these terms it elaborates a whole system, measuring and marking out borders and defining all the relations it finds on its path. By this means, it seeks to go as far as possible—which, in light of the poverty it has inflicted on itself, is not far. Then, satisfied with its efforts, it simply stays put and never considers anything, no matter how obvious its utility may be, except for everyday categories, fully confident that it has resisted drawing analogies between sensory and non-sensory relations and is observing the true, scientific method. But for all that, it only manages to arrive at a picture through analogies in the first place, for every symbol, or schema, represents something immaterial in material form.

Essentially, philosophy has arbitrarily declared that no analogies or schemata other than the ones it has deemed proper may be employed for naming and explaining non-sensory concepts. It authorizes the schema of inside/outside, without which it can do nothing at all, but as soon as someone uses the model of center/periphery to capture a relationship, it casts a sidelong glance and mutters, "So that's how it's going to be. . . ." Yet if it is licit to express a simple relationship between two non-sensory items through the spatial image of inside/outside (for instance, when one concept is included within the broader scope of the other)—indeed, even if it's impossible not to do so—why, then, is it prohibited to formulate the same state of affairs in terms of center/periphery? The latter schema is not any more spatial than inside/outside; it is a more exact articulation of the relationship and enhances definition and detail; just as there are complex figures in space, highly convoluted relations exist in realms not given to the senses—in the mind, for example. One would only be able to capture a relationship between two non-sensory things that implied inside and outside with a series of circumlocutions that ultimately offered the mind nothing but a bunch of disjointed symbols; and if connections between parts are jumbled, an unclear view of the matter is the result. So why, if there's no representing a complex relationship clearly without schemata, shouldn't one find a comparison that expresses nuances directly? Just take the psychological studies we have and see how spatial symbolism is necessary for depicting how various forces act on each other, since the essence of one faculty is manifest only in light of others. Psychic components are pictured in, next to, above, below, and against each other; some of them reflect, others store, still others connect—and who knows what else. These same images are so mixed up and thrown-together without reference to each other that it's difficult to see how an integrated model of psychic life could ever emerge. Half of them are taken from one sphere, and half from another, without fitting together at all, and the result is supposed to offer a "scientific account." Why not elucidate the overall context all at once with unified symbolism corresponding to the unified nature of what is being discussed?

In the following, the question remains open whether the mode of representation is correct; it would be wrong to think that one may do as one will with symbols. Still, I submit for consideration one possible application of the principles outlined above.—

The psyche is a circle, and its rays (mental actions) run from a midpoint (the faculty of reason) toward the periphery (sensory perception, or the outer limit of the soul) and work beyond it, for the periphery is located within a larger circle (the external world of sensible phenomena); by the same token, but conversely, the larger circle (the external world) gains in concentration as it approaches the inner circle (sensory periphery/outer limit of the soul) and, in so doing, acts upon the midpoint.*

This picture—which can be developed at greater length—presents the most general relations of psychic life clearly enough; I say "most general" because a more detailed account would require a more detailed symbol. The absolute unity of immaterial reason stands in contrast to the senses, which border on and coincide with the world of sense (for the world of sense exists for us only insofar as it is apprehended by the senses); the senses take up the manifold of the external world *idealiter* (the rays of the larger circle, which propagate their effect through the periphery to the center of the psychic circle), so that no effect from outside can penetrate the soul except by sensory perception, which consists of the radially concentrated pressure of the external world on the periphery. The opposing but complementary thrust of mental activity is illustrated here by rays that stretch in two directions at once; rays from the external world reach into the circle (continuing in the direction in which they strike the periphery, toward the center) and become ideational, or cognitive, action; rays from the center toward the periphery extend and work beyond this border as volitional action;

* That is, if the circle reaches outward, to the external world, by extending its rays to all sides, and, at the same time, the external world converges upon it, then the circle's periphery must be the point of intersection for both. The pressure from without is felt, via the periphery, throughout the whole circle; conversely, the smaller circle's pressure on the larger circle—the external world—propagates itself *virtualiter* beyond the periphery. Consider that when two people are moving toward each other from opposite directions, each feels the pressure of the other without any energy passing between them *realiter*. May no one mistake influence through the periphery (outward or inward) for an arbitrary assertion on my part.

accordingly, reason, the midpoint, can be viewed from two angles: on the one hand, it takes in the rays from the external world and, in the process, coincides with pure consciousness; on the other hand, it emits purposeful rays effecting acts of will.—Of the spheres to which the psyche is connected, the body certainly comes first; the psyche exerts influence first and foremost on physical substance, and through physical organs it receives the raw material of its representations; however, the sphere of the body is located within a larger sphere, the external world, and consequently, in terms of the most elementary symbolism, an array of concentric circles emerges, one encompassing the other.

This symbol could, basically, be expanded at will; in order to follow mental operations in detail, a higher order of symbol would be necessary; I intend to demonstrate, in another essay, the lines along which such inquiry would have to proceed. In all likelihood, the undertaking leads to heights that mathematics has not attained to date, and inasmuch as the bodily sphere would necessarily expand in parallel to the psychic one, I am convinced that the most fully developed symbol for the human soul would ultimately overlap with the form and proportions of the human body, such that the former amounted to the intellectual reflection of the latter. I will also show that the body really can be developed along these same symbolic lines; indeed, this is the case for everything organic.

Until then, I will leave it open, whether and to what extent the symbol chosen is accurate; on one point or the other, it might already appear deficient: the divisions between psychic forces that we have been making cannot be seen in the symbol, because they are not materially given; indeed, in my opinion, the divisions to be made should follow *a priori* from the symbol itself. So this symbol might be the wrong one. At any rate, I have merely sought to show the possibility of using One Image to illustrate clearly what throwing together many images only confuses.

The mode of representation defended here belongs to natural philosophy, which has deep, spiritual roots; misuse should not be blamed on the science itself but on parties who act without adequate knowledge of the symbol and the nature of symbolism; those who cannot steer the light it casts only inflict harm. When vulgar philosophy sets out to explain—or better, since it does not presume quite that much, to describe—the psyche, it takes a bit of vegetable matter, some part of the human being, a geometrical line, and some of this, that, or the other, then stitches them all together to make a picture; but a natural philosopher takes the plant, the person, the sphere, or whatever it is he wishes to demonstrate, and shows its very soul. The ordinary philosopher demolishes a host of integral symbols in order to recreate the whole from heterogeneous elements. The natural philosopher takes what he finds in its entirety and reveals that fullness of the object. The former fails to see the tree for the forest; he chops away, makes beams, carves branches and twigs, and sees how far he can get with the dead matter he has assembled; when the latter arrives at the scene, he laughs at his counterpart and asks him why he has hacked down all the trees just to make one of his own—after all, he could have kept what was already standing there.

The ordinary philosopher will think his companion is full of hot air—or drink. Now, it is true that natural philosophers speak in other tongues. I could say that they do so because the Holy Spirit has descended upon them—that they no longer know the language of the pharisaical philosophers and book-learned, but are speaking the language of the world itself and will one day impart it with their wisdom. However, I prefer to be honest and admit that natural philosophers do not fully understand the foreign tongues they speak; a fair share of fantasy has poured from their wine. Yet this wine is noble. Those for whom it is too heady should not imbibe nectar in which the finest sap of the whole vine has fermented—not just drops of water pressed from some mangled shoot. To be sure, some natural philosophers working the field are clumsy, and some of them start building without laying a solid foundation; but if this is the case, they still wish what they are making to reach the heavens, and only because they cannot wait to see it soar do they rush; in spite of the debris that is constantly falling, the design itself has divine proportions. Natural philosophy is prone to reverie, but only because it recognizes that truth, as much as beauty, is a matter of unity. Cast out the water, but not the newborn babe; though babbling for the moment, the child already shows the traits of one who will rule the world.

In essence, the new philosophy permits infinitely different representations of the same thing, and thus it achieves what other philosophies cannot: it elucidates its object both for those striving for the highest insight and those who move in a lower sphere and are unable to apprehend what is too abstract for them; this philosophy will not belong to one caste standing apart from the rest of humanity because of superior knowledge, but circulate freely, available to low and high born in equal measure; for it adapts to the mind and character of anyone and everyone, affirming inner truth and dignity for all. For one who wishes to know the state of scientific progress, it will provide the mathematical symbol, either as a formula or in spatial articulation, the ultimate schema or sign from which all others must necessarily derive if they are to count as true. In this way, mathematical schemata will regulate the use of more concrete symbols, which will prevent them from being degraded into idle talk. He who has grasped these absolute, universal symbols will be in the position to instruct the people according to the abstract schema supplied by mathematics, which he will put into more tangible terms with a sure and steady hand. As matters stand today, one material thing is used to symbolize another. While not inherently worthy of blame, this method remains uncertain so long as *concreta* cannot be shown to derive from a higher and more abstract order.

Once the solid foundation underlying such abstract symbols is established, it will be possible to speak philosophically with men of all estates, in their own tongue. The lawfulness of the universe will be demonstrated to the statesman by way of the political machine he steers, to the physiologist the human body, to the natural scientist crystals and plants, to the artist the empire of colors and tones, to the shoemaker the shoe, and to the farmer the field and plough. All proportions—the Absolute, which those at the pinnacle of learning endeavor to know—will be made plain and clear on the basis of insight into fundamental laws of mathematical schemata, translated into formulas capturing concrete facts as they fall under a general heading.—Just as the equation $x^2 + y^2 = r^2$ applies to all circles and allows any value to be supplied for x and y, it will be possible to group vast arrays of things together and substitute different values in a unified scheme.

There's no doubting that natural philosophy, at its present state of development, is more a method than a system; however, it harbors the potential for a system of the highest order inasmuch as it anticipates, and seeks to prove, the strict, universal principle of oneness. To date, it has observed the general rule that, for any science wishing to merit its title, all things must obey One Principle, and in this spirit has it acted; in truth, doing so already represents an accomplishment of real magnitude.

ON THE RELATIONSHIP BETWEEN ART, SCIENCE, AND RELIGION

Since human beings can recognize nothing in itself and their knowledge concerns only proportions and relations between one thing and another, I believe that seeking out and representing connections between the item of interest and others in the same sphere will prove more availing than explanations based on so-called *realia*; for usually—nay, always—such relations are what determines the particularity of the object in question. This approach strikes me as all the more necessary given that proximate concepts and terms, whose relative independence is maintained by definitions, do not occupy a position alongside each other so much as they overlap and interpenetrate in organic fashion (that is, their relations are reciprocal) so that if in defining one term reference to the other is omitted, need arises to incorporate elements of the latter into one's understanding of the former, even as it remains impossible to make the relationship between the two clear.

In the broadest sense, science, art, and religion are the three realms that constitute the sphere of human activity we call "life"—by which I do not mean just bare, physical existence. In subjective terms, I would define these realms as follows. *Science* is the representation (or, from another point of view, the possession) of a multitude of insights in the form of a whole that coheres according to logical rules; *art* is the free production of something purposeful;

and *religion* is the belief, also evident in practical actions, in what reason demands be accepted as the foundation of moral law. With that, I have offered characteristics that allow each realm to be distinguished from the others, but the essential Form, which follows from how these realms determine each other, remains hidden.

But if I explain science in reference to art and religion, I am not just offering the most substantive definition that can be made, since all that is real and admits understanding amounts to relations between neighboring realms, and this is the very essence of knowledge—a definition that expresses the whole essence of science; I am also providing a definition that makes it possible to survey the entirety of the sphere and the relationship to the whole of which science forms a part. Admittedly, we are incapable of conceiving relations and proportions in anything but schematic or symbolic terms, and if we express the whole sphere of human activity through a symbol, then it will only be possible to express components and aspects of this sphere through corresponding components and aspects of the symbol, because only in this way can the relationships and relations of the same, inasmuch as they agree and bring forth the whole sphere, emerge clearly.

To be sure, it seems one might avoid symbols, at least in part, by saying, for instance: "The essence of *science* consists of recognizing and representing the particular on the basis of the general, the individual on the basis of the whole;* the essence of *art* is to recognize and represent the general in light of the particular, the whole in light of the individual; the essence of *religion* involves recognizing and representing the relation between one whole, or general principle, and a higher whole, or general principle (that is, something

* *General* refers to the content of concepts, and *whole* to their scope and, thus, the objects within their purview.

larger with regard to which it appears distinct or particular)." However, this definition, because it contains several expressions stripped of symbolic content, proves very empty, undetermined, and in need of filling-in, since one can imagine the relations to be captured only inasmuch as thought substitutes particular figures for general expressions, which leaves a wide berth for arbitrariness; precisely because this definition permits such free substitution, I would reserve it for symbolism of a more specific kind. If only in passing, let me remind the reader that I understand "religion" here neither as positive religion nor as a dead system of belief, but as it ought to be in keeping with the nature of things—or, since I can pronounce judgment only within the compass of my own views, how it ought to be (a point on which I will elaborate below); moreover, that "science" does not refer to endeavor (that is, to study), but to knowledge attained, the essence of which is the conscious possession of the general.

Not only is there scientific, artistic, and religious knowledge; per the distinction introduced by the words *know* and *represent*, corresponding forms of activity exist. Scientific knowledge begins where artistic knowledge stops, and vice-versa. Where the psychic and physical faculties of the artist come into play in a passive capacity, those of the scientist do so actively, as the examples illustrating the definition will show, for science aims for the particular (to be real, each science must already have the general for purposes of deduction) and then represents it, if it has not yet been attained, or observes it, if it truly is depicted as from the general; art proceeds in the opposite direction, coming to rest when it has portrayed the general through the particular.

Say I have a plant before me; there is nothing for me to do here in an artistic capacity; inasmuch as I wish to entertain a relationship with the plant as an artist, I need only take in the character of the whole plant, its general impression, by means of so-called artistic intuition; for the researcher, in contrast, there is need for scientific activity: he must disarticulate the plant into discrete parts in order to arrive at knowledge of the particular in it, where he then stops, in contemplation. If the material constituting the plant were already given in particular, the scientist would have nothing more to examine, he could be content simply to observe it; an artist, on the other hand, would have to take this disparate matter and fashion it into a whole by bringing each discrete element into relation to the idea of the integral plant.

The scientist will break apart a statue in order to see what kind of stone it is made from, or analyze it mentally to see whether a given muscle starts at the right place, is lying and extending properly, and so on; but the artist takes in the idea of the whole as he stands there and contemplates it. The scientist observes the block of raw marble and its veins, whereas the artist takes a chisel in hand. For a group of workmen, the whole is given in the activity itself; each person takes part and contributes something particular or specialized. The artist attends to the activity in its entirety; in his eyes, each individual is important only to the extent that he contributes to the overall effect; the scientist, for his part, sees value in the activity only insofar as he can identify the sensibility, or deeper motivations, of each of the parties involved (which he seeks to discern on the basis of the concerted effort); when the character traits of several people are plain, the scientist has nothing more to do. But the artist will fashion them into a whole—be it a novel, a drama, or even a polity. Such are their respective stances with regard to all circumstances and conditions of life.

As far as religion is concerned, the following example is illustrative.

Our organism consists of individual organs that are complete in themselves; on the one hand, they lead an independent life in the larger whole, and on the other hand they are inseparable components of the same. The heart, lungs, liver, and brain are all, so to speak, individual animals with their own unique way of living; each one draws sustenance from a general source, the blood, and in turn emits a substance particular to itself (corresponding to secretions of the body as a whole); all the same, the various organs are subordinate to the overall organism. Each component entertains a specific relation with the whole that may not be violated, lest the organism in its entirety—and indirectly the organ itself—suffer damage. For instance, were the heart unwilling to perform its duty of moving the blood, or the liver loath to discharge bile, it would disrupt the health of the overall organism and, indirectly, its own wellbeing, for the organism would now be unable to provide for these organs adequately; likewise, if the lungs, which only need to take in a certain amount of blood, were so self-centered as to lay claim to an inordinate quantity of the same, they would temporarily display heightened vitality (inflammation), but by disrupting the lawfulness of the organism they might induce its death, and with that their own—or some other ill redounding to their disadvantage.

The essence of an organism is not that it consists of a liver, lungs, heart, and so on (as is the case for human beings). Rather, it is a matter of the reciprocal action through which each part exists thanks to the whole and, conversely, the whole exists thanks to discrete components. Moreover, not just the body, but also the soul is a whole of this kind; so is every polity—the estates are its various organs; so is humanity, the realm of all living beings on our planet, the solar system, indeed, the very cosmos. Whatever exists, exists though interaction, as part of a larger whole—a progression that readily admits elaboration. Thus, not only is every little cellular lobule (*acinus*) of the liver part of a larger whole—of the liver, first and foremost, from which its functions are inseparable—and not only is the liver in its entirety a part of a greater unity, namely the integral human being; in like manner, each human being belongs to a larger body, namely humankind, which in turn forms part of a greater unity, i.e., nature as it exists in our solar system (or, more precisely, as it exists on earth—or, more precisely still, as per the kingdom of manifold organisms inhabiting it), and so on, *ad infinitum*. At each point, analogous interaction occurs between the higher and lower whole, whereby neither can neglect the other without damaging itself. Admittedly, the individual human being is not connected with humankind—or, more specifically, with the state (which represents a more directly superordinate instance)—through membranous tissue, as the liver is connected to our body. But whether attachments are made by skin or some other means has no bearing on the essence of organic bonds.

In my view, religion is not a matter of praying or singing, nor does it concern dead belief. In part, it is knowledge of the relationship we entertain with the whole to which we belong; in essence, it is a matter of recognizing our duties and how we may prove useful. Equally, religion involves making this relationship a reality, that is, doing what our relation to the whole demands; the first is religious knowledge, the second religious action. All of morality must derive from the connection between the part and the higher, organic whole; this relationship pervades the world in its entirety. If, in the following, I take the human organism as the symbol for illustrating the general law of the organic whole, I do so for the sake of clarity—to avoid bandying about words that seem too abstract—and because it represents the point of reference with which I am most familiar.

Why must one being sacrifice itself for the common good? When a muscle allows itself to be absorbed because its relationship to the organism dictates this necessity, it's true that its individuality is destroyed for the moment, yet it will soon emerge again, in another form, from the bodily mass into which it has dissolved. The muscle will regain individuality, and, in its new guise, be better off; because it allowed itself to be absorbed and destroyed *qua* individual, it has promoted the health of the organism; if it had resisted this process, and thereby acted to general disadvantage, it would—after finally having dissolved, after all—find itself reconstituted in a worse state, since the overall organism had suffered, too. Human beings must sacrifice themselves for the common good for their own sake. After death, one reemerges with a new, independent individuality; having acted, in the previous life, to the detriment of the world, one now suffers in one's new condition as a result. Every misstep includes its own punishment, for all interference with general rights backfires on the wrongdoer either right away or at some point down the line. Does this mean one should act in a religious manner simply for one's own sake? It strikes me as pure self-interest, egoism that no longer deserves such a hateful name, since no one can achieve blessedness by means other than working toward that of one's fellow organs (that is, fellow human beings).

Virtue, it follows, is viewing oneself as a member of the greater whole and acting as such; vice is seeking to establish oneself as the whole and trying to set its other parts in one's own service. All virtue is simply self-sacrifice, and vice egoism. Conscience is the direct feeling—like an instinct, I submit—that by violating our relations to the whole, of which we form parts, we are indirectly damaging ourselves; in the body, the counterpart of a bad conscience is pain; a bad conscience is moral pain. All law, right, and justice has its foundation here. If someone acts egoistically, with no regard for his relationship to the collective, and instead wishes everything to be about him alone, then the other members of the group have the obligation to stand in his way, because such self-centeredness necessarily makes the collective suffer.

But the most general relation between the individual and the whole involves seeking one's weal in the preservation of the group. In organic life, the state, humankind, and the world itself, then, law and order find more perfect realization in proportion to the more truly things are lawfully ordered. Should one organ in our body try to expand at the expense of other parts or claim vital fluids in excess of the amount assigned by the organism as a whole, then all other organs will work against its doing so; this is the so-called healing power inherent in nature. In the state, this is where the law properly intervenes; in a broader perspective, wars ensure the balance between the organs of humankind; in a still bigger picture, we can see the application of justice at least in part—since we are denied a synoptic, cosmic view—when, for example, the number of caterpillars gets out of hand and a flock of birds descends to make sure they do not continue to multiply.

By fundamental rights, no one may seek to use his fellow man to the detriment of the collective; no obligation exists toward the particular, but only toward the whole; this ensures that neither too much nor too little is done for one member or another. The distinction between higher and lower duties, those closer and those more distant, follows as a matter of course—as does the conflict that may arise between them. Lobules have an immediate obligation to the liver to which they belong most directly; correspondingly, human beings have an obligation to the state to which they belong; a more remote duty concerns the organism as a whole: lobules must serve the body, of which the liver forms part, and people must do the same with regard to humankind. Duty to the integral organism stands higher than duty to the liver, duty to the human race surpasses duty to the state. In a perfect organism—which, admittedly, exists only as an Idea—each organ performs its lower and higher duties simultaneously; by acting for the benefit of the greater unity that encompasses it most directly, an organ acts in the best possible manner for the greater whole that includes lesser wholes. But in an organism where individual wholes revolt against the greater whole, lesser wholes may ask: "Should we follow immediate or higher duty? Should I act against the weal of my state for the sake of humanity, against the good of my family for the state—or the opposite?" The former is to be affirmed.

Incidentally, one can relate religious modes of knowledge and action—like those of art and science—to various objects directly. To take up the previous example, say that I am considering a plant. In essence, religious knowledge, insofar as one can speak of its bearing on a plant, concerns its relationship to the Idea of the whole of nature (or to that of the integral state, to which human being and plant life belong), and realizing this relationship as fully as possible: cultivating its growth or eradicating it in keeping with the wellbeing of the greater whole.

Following this perhaps overly long digression—which was introduced in part to refute the claim that natural philosophy has nothing to do with morality and therefore amounts to a one-sided endeavor—let me return to our threefold definition.

Often, science is explained in relation to the notion of principle; this is not the case for art and religion. While one might declare that science involves examining and representing a manifold phenomenon according to a principle, one would not say that art is a matter of representing a principle in manifold form. This might seem strange since, if "principle" were just another name for, or a symbolic expression of, the general *per se*, art and religion could be explained just as well as science in relation to it. However, "principle" is a symbolic expression for the general only insofar as the relationship at issue is conceived in scientific terms; that is, the word refers to something general that counts as a starting point from which one proceeds in order to arrive at an assortment of particulars. Because this relationship is found specifically in science, the expression "principle" applies only here. (That said, and strictly speaking, one shouldn't explain science in explicit reference to principle, since it is only through scientific explanation that the term can be made clear and differentiated from the general *per se*, or from other symbols in use.)

Just as "principle" refers to the general in science, "idea" refers to the general in relation to art: something general that one conceives in the particular taken as a whole or seeks to incorporate into a particular phenomenon (in other words, to represent by way of the particular). Accordingly, if I represent the idea of abiding virtue through individual characters and events, I am looking, artistically, at the idea of a general human course of action in the doings of one particular person. In religion, the general also has a specific name: God. To posit religious relationships in broad terms, one invokes God, the highest and most general Truth, so that the generalities He contains within Himself may be recognized and known.

Our highest duties, but also those that are most remote, are directed toward God; however, the greatest duty is best fulfilled in mediated fashion, by performing the duty closest at hand; indeed, there is no other way to discharge the highest of obligations. The fullest service rendered unto God occurs in one's immediate surroundings, even when acting in His service runs counter to their wellbeing. Commonly, what we call "God" is anthropomorphized and attributed qualities borrowed from the sphere of human activity, just with the predicate "general" attached; this is not blameworthy, but it beseems those who do so not to hunt down, draw the sword against, or threaten with fire other modes of representation; their own ways rely on symbolism in the same measure.

If—as sometimes occurs, and not just in a religious context—one wishes to call God the *most general* and the *most absolute*, it is possible to define the ideal of science and art in reference to God. Then, science is knowledge and representation of how the particular constituents of the world have emerged from Him; art is knowledge and representation of the divine in the earthly realm (parts of the world belonging to our immediate proximity); and religion is the knowledge and fulfillment of our duties to God.

As many different symbolic explanations of art and science can be provided as there are symbols for general and particular modes of relation: an infinite number. If, in a given whole, what is particular to it is called *matter*, and the way this particular stuff is combined is called *form*, then I can say: science considers only the form of the whole inasmuch as it relates to matter; art considers matter insofar as it relates to form; and religion is the whole itself: matter for making the form of greater unity.

For science, the essential task is to find and represent all the peripheral points surrounding a given focal point; for art, to find the focal point of a circle on the basis of peripheral points, or to posit a center by giving form to its periphery; for religion, to view the focal point of any given circle as a point on the periphery of another center and to make it stand forth as such relative to other peripheral points. Consider the illustration below:

Here, the midpoint symbolizes the general, which also belongs to all peripheral points symbolizing the particular.

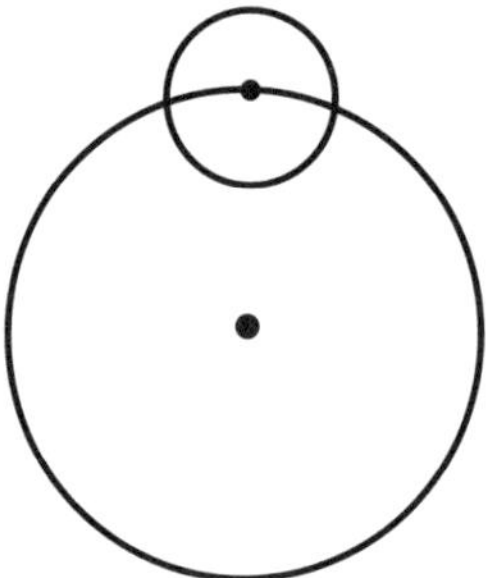

Insofar as the periphery is described from the center outward, the center represents a *principle*; but if the center is described by the periphery, that is, if the formation of the periphery posits the center, as it were, the center represents an *idea*; finally, if a center is posited as a peripheral point of a higher center, where a limit fixed at a level shared with other peripheral points restricts its further elaboration, this higher center is *God*.

Or, if we posit a symbol for an infinite series—for instance—

$a + a^2 + a^3 + a^4 + \text{etc.},$

then we can say: science finds and represents all particular values of the series from the general law of the series, whether determined on the basis of the recurring element or its exponents; art, conversely, recognizes the general law of the series through its particular values or presents it to the senses by putting together particular elements (finite fragments of an infinite progression); and religion teaches us to view the sum total of the infinite series as part of a greater, infinite series to whose law it is subordinated.

Scientific cosmogony starts with the sun, from which it lets particular planets be born; artistic cosmogony begins with the planets, and the sun emerges through their concerted action, in the center; religion, which looks down from a higher standpoint, unifies both science and art and elaborates the entire system of sun and planets in reference to another, more exalted star.

Science breaks the integral ray of light into manifold colors; art brings the colors together into the spectrum (not the unified beam of light, which symbolizes the idea, but its components, discrete and unfused); religion treats the whole chromatic spectrum as the broken beam of a universal light illuminating the world, with our senses—hearing, smell, sentiment, and so forth—attuned to its prismatic rays.

At this juncture, the Symbol of the Circle merits further analysis.

Nothing is arbitrary in science apart from the object to which the scientific principle is applied; if one has the center, then only the length of the radius remains left to my discretion, and once the latter has been established, the totality of individual points on the periphery follows as a matter of course; the radius describing the periphery provides the thread of deduction: how the particular depends on the general; as soon as one abandons this reference, presuming to find a peripheral point though guesswork or approximation, one gets lost, and even the keenest senses prove unavailing. Whatever is true lies at the same distance from the center as all other points on the periphery, which belong to the world of the particular. Consequently, it is possible for something to be true in one respect but false in another. A hare twenty feet long would not occur in the external world; such an entity is unavailable to the senses, at the outer periphery, but it stands available to the inner, peripheral sphere of mental representation and therefore truly exists within its compass. The truth does not admit degrees, but is a matter of occupying the same space relative to the center. There are multiple ways of knowing, that is, methods for arriving at knowledge, or, in terms of the symbol, means of obtaining a circle. The so-called scientific method, properly speaking, is synthetic: it deduces all particulars from the general, and nothing constrains the process of derivation; hereby, a point that is infinitely intensive at the outset extends to all sides; no fixed limit determines how far the center may expand, and each periphery that is produced becomes the "mother" of a still-larger periphery: a general principle commands an array of subordinate, particular principles, which in turn are general insofar as they command others grouped under them; knowledge increases at uniform distances from the center. There is another method, the analytical, which would seem to go from the particular to the general and float between the scientific and artistic approaches; its symbolism is not the center stretching outward and creating a periphery, but the radius orbiting a central point and forming arcs that together describe the whole of the periphery.

Were the periphery produced without the mediation of the radius, this method would be altogether artistic; it qualifies as scientific because it possessed the general beforehand, that is, it did not determine the center through the periphery only to conceal the radius—through which it makes each individual point, or particular, dependent on the center, or general—so that, admittedly, it seems to the neophyte that the particular reveals the general; this method is for students; if it is to have scientific unity, the teacher's whole analytical depiction must be developed from a principle already known. Science does not have a free hand with the analytical method, for the length of the radius it posits is valid only for a certain, particular area; if more is to be derived from the same center, the field needs to be expanded by the synthetic method. Here, a third method comes into play, that of natural philosophy, which does not find the periphery it seeks through an actual radius, in the direction of which a center (principle) then expands, or which revolves around a center; rather, it finds the periphery through another periphery already given and concentric to it by applying rules of scale—for the analogies employed by natural philosophy are nothing but qualitative proportions—and in this manner, starting from arbitrarily chosen segments of a known sphere, it finds segments of an unknown sphere by correlating one point in the first with a corresponding point in the second. The proportions reach beyond what any actual radius can attain; natural philosophy constructs its peripheries *a priori*, according to formulas; in order to arrive at a wholly new peripheral sphere, just One Radius is needed, which represents more than the many radii the other methods need. Indeed, natural philosophy does not require an empirically given periphery to find the one it seeks; simply through the length of the radius—that is, on the principle of the relation between one particular point in the whole of what is sought and the center point—it can find the periphery in its entirety. Natural philosophy infers that the brain corresponds to the human organism as the sun does to the system of planets. Needless to say, should the premise be false, or if the relation between the initial terms is not well enough understood, the results will prove strange—as is often the case. But one day natural philosophy will demonstrate mathematical certainty and represent, as it were, a qualitative mathematics.

Science has the center and sets out to create the periphery from here. Art proceeds in the opposite manner: it makes a freehand drawing of the periphery in order to make the midpoint that it posits visible. A given midpoint admits representation through an infinite number of peripheries, greater or smaller in size; thus, each and every idea allows for a limitless array of artistic designs. How many ways are there to portray the battle between virtue and vice, for instance? To be able to create a midpoint by delineating the periphery, the artist must actually see, in his mind's eye, the idea he would make manifest. The ultimate demand of a work of art is that all parts should contribute, in equal measure, to making available to the senses the core idea, to which each point of the periphery (the manifold of elements) owes its existence. If one were to draw first legs, then a torso and head, without a clear idea of how they fit together, how monstrous would the creation be? Likewise, to write an act in a play without knowing what will come in the next one is to proceed haphazardly, in the mere hope that a focus will emerge on its own.

Work in view of the idea is the rule of the artist's craft: the radius he draws in spirit at every point. Artistic genius not only has conceived the midpoint at which it aims, but has also drawn, mentally, the whole periphery around it—or, better, it always sees the midpoint through and in a periphery that is already complete, and it traces sure and definite lines according to this mental image. Lesser talents have only the center, the idea; they work in reference to it, but haltingly, because for each part of the periphery they draw, they must gauge the distance from the center, as it were, to see whether it fits with the rest; in contrast, a genius knows nothing of the midpoint without having already pictured the completed circle around it. An object is beautiful insofar as it fits into a peripheral arrangement that makes a rounded center perfectly manifest to the senses, in which it is then perceived by the public. Accordingly, it is possible for something that would be beautiful in one work of art to appear ugly in another: part of a perfect circle placed in another figure of greater or lesser diameter disrupts the harmony inasmuch as it doesn't fit. But whatever seems to belong to a larger circle than the one we occupy and lets us sense this greater whole, is sublime. Hence the peculiar sensation that the sublime provokes: we feel the proximity of a world greater than the narrow one we inhabit, yet we cannot compass its dimensions. That which is sublime for us is beautiful for the Higher Beings taking in, with an all-encompassing gaze, what is given to us only in part. In my view, the circle is not just the symbol of beauty; everything in nature that is truly beautiful must represent an evolution of the circle or, more precisely, the sphere. (Space prohibits elaborating on the matter at this juncture.)

Take the following figure:

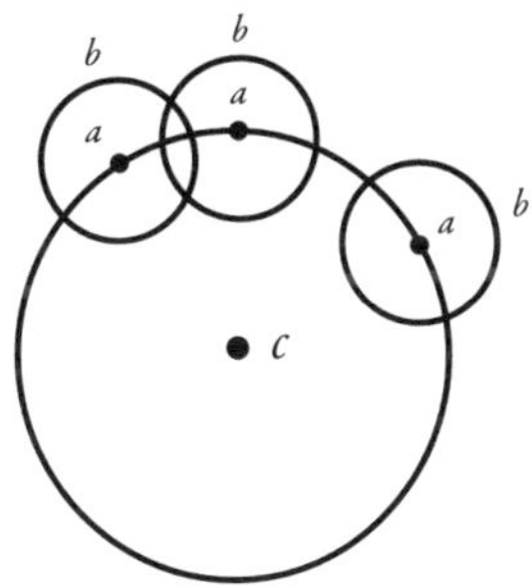

Let point *a* stand for a human being. As far as he can see in his surroundings, he views himself as the center of periphery *b*; religion, however, teaches that he is only a point along a larger periphery, which depends on *c*; he is told to comport himself accordingly—that if he steps outside his appointed sphere, the lawfulness of the whole will be disturbed; each point adjacent to his own has just as much inherent value as he does, and it stands just as close to point *c*, which is paramount (that is, God); all points owe their condition and continued existence to holding and acting together; each one occupies its place in the arrangement, and is but a meaningless dot without it.

Point *a* may extend its periphery outward, but the same is permitted to every other point, as well; accordingly, the periphery that each point forms around itself reaches into that of other points; this constitutes the interaction between them; if each one expands more or less equally, then nothing occurs to the detriment of the circle as a whole; but should one of them wish for immoderate expansion relative to the others—forgetting the summit from which they all depend and seeking to elevate itself to a position above others—then imbalance results.

It will be clear that these elementary symbols admit considerable expansion; indeed, they can be developed along lines enabling us to express far more nuanced relations than those provided here—the implications of which will be explored in the final essay.

FRAGMENT FROM THE SYMBOLISM OF CONIC SECTIONS

The discussion here and in the following portion of the book bears, in part, only on matters presented in the preceding pages. That all three chapters have little in common with standard mathematics will already be plain: they have found a place in the volume at hand.

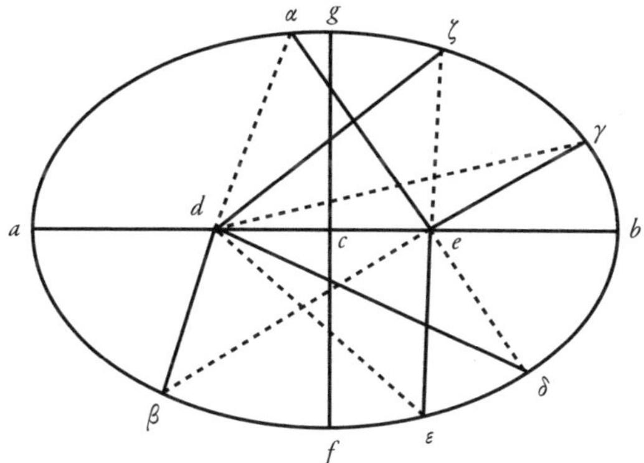

An ellipse is a figure of the shape depicted above, containing two points, *d* and *e* (called *foci*), which are defined by the fact that all broken lines (e.g., *dαe*, *dζe*, *dδe*, etc.) extending from one focus to an arbitrary point of the circumference (e.g., *α*, *β*, *γ*, *δ*, *ε*, *ζ*, etc.) and back to the other focus are together equal in length to *ab*, which passes through both foci to the circumference and constitutes the major axis. The point *c*, which lies in the middle of the major axis, is the midpoint of the ellipses, and its foci stand at an equal distance to either side; the farther they lie from it, and the closer to the circumference, the greater the sideways length of the ellipse appears. The line *fg* extending to the circumference, drawn vertically through the midpoint on the major axis, is called the minor axis. One curious feature of elliptical form is that, if one places a light or utters a word at one focal point in the elliptical curvature, the rays of light or sound waves, in keeping with how they strike the circumference, will travel to the other focus; that is, even if one speaks softly at one focal point, a person standing at the other point (no matter how distant) will hear the words clearly, because all the sounds come back together here. It is well known that the planets describe an elliptical course with the sun at one of the foci.

If one pictures both foci of an ellipse moving toward each other, as the circumference of the ellipse draws together in proportion to the convergence of the foci, then the longish form of the figure will come closer and closer to assuming a round shape; indeed, if both foci coincide completely and the circumference adjusts correspondingly, the ellipse will become a perfect circle; conversely, one can picture an ellipse emerging from a circle if its midpoint splits apart in opposing directions, and the circumference expands proportionately in these same directions. Just as one can imagine a circle as an ellipse in which the focal points overlap, one can picture an ellipse as a circle with a midpoint that has divided into two focal points. That said, mathematics retains only the first variant.

The properties of the circle are familiar. All lines drawn from the midpoint (center) to a point on the circumference (periphery)—or vice versa, from the circumference to the midpoint—are equal to each other and called radii. The rays from a light source placed at the midpoint of a circle (or, more precisely, a spherical space), when they strike the peripheral wall, will be reflected back to the center.

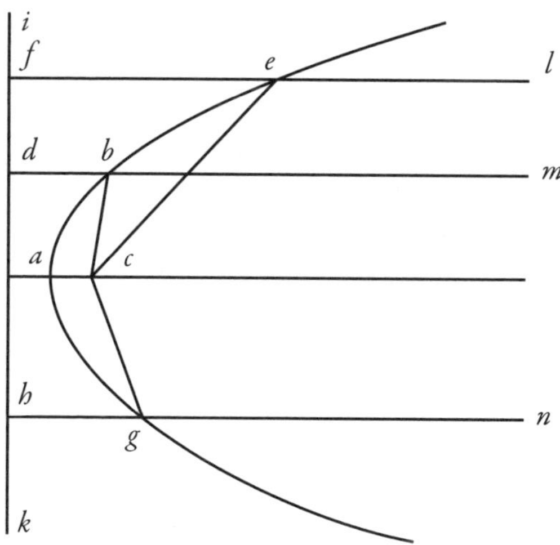

A parabola is a line as represented above, with branches that must be pictured as extending forever, since they do not form a closed figure (as in a circle or ellipse). The focus, *c*, has the particularity that each line (*cb*, *cg*, *ce*, etc.) that can be drawn to a given part of the circumference is as large as a line drawn vertically from the same point on the circumference to *ik*—a line outside the parabola called the *directrix*; that is, *cg* is equal to *gh*, *cb* to *bd*, *ce* to *ef*, and so on. The line drawn vertically through the focus parallel to the directrix is called the *axis* of the parabola, and two times the distance from the focus to the directrix is called the parabola's *parameter*. If a light source is placed at the focal point of a parabolic curvature, all rays that strike the circumference (*cb*, *ce*, *cg*, and so on) are thrown back parallel to the axis (to *el*, *bm*, *gn*) and would only intersect at a measureless remove—insofar as mathematicians assume that parallel lines meet up at infinity. For this reason, the parabola can be viewed mathematically as an ellipse, but with a second focus lying at an infinite distance from focus *c*. Were light rays from the first focus to strike *e*, *b*, or *g* and traverse infinity, they would all meet up again in the second focus, as occurs with an ellipse. Similarly, but in reverse, one can picture rays coming from a focal point at an infinite remove striking the inner curvature of the parabola and converging at focus *c*.—Any object thrown by hand describes (if we disregard air resistance) a section of a parabolic arc.

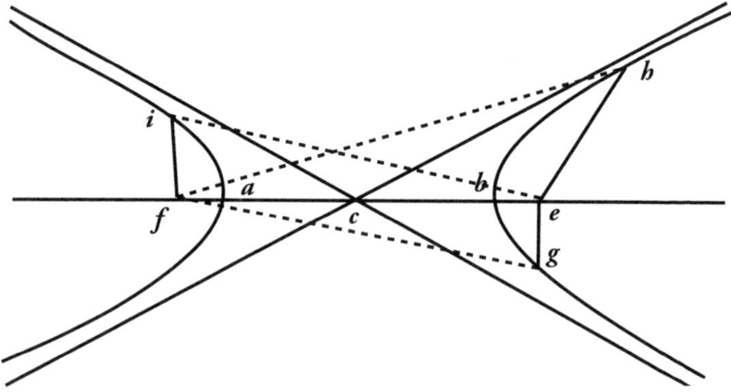

The hyperbola is a strange line, which can never exist in its own right. Invariably, the formation of one hyperbola coincides with the formation of another hyperbola as its mirror image; both hyperbolas belong together as inseparably as two halves of an ellipse divided by the minor axis (but visibly merging with each other). Each hyperbola has its own focus: *e* and *f*. Here, something peculiar arises: take any two lines (*fg* and *ge*, *fh* and *he*, or *ei* and *if*, etc.), drawing the first from the focus of one hyperbola (*f*) to a point in the curve of the other hyperbola (*g*, *h*), and the second from this point of incidence (*g* or *h*) going to the other focus (*e*); one line exceeds the other by a distance equal to the major axis (*ab*); the difference between all such lines is equal to the major axis. As with a parabola, the branches of the hyperbola extend infinitely. Two straight lines pictured running crosswise through the midpoint of the hyperbola, *c*, as shown in the figure, are called its *asymptotes*; they have the curious feature of drawing closer and closer to the branches of the hyperbola but never (at least within the compass of what we can conceive) meeting up with them, except in infinity. If a light is placed at the focus of a hyperbolic curve, the rays are bent in divergent manner, whereas they are convergent in an ellipse, parallel in a parabola, and bounce back on themselves in a circle. At the same time, this divergence occurs in such a way that, if one imagines the bent rays extending to the hyperbola opposite, they would all intersect in the latter's focus. One can also picture both hyperbolas as emerging from an ellipse, if, in the mathematical formula for the figure of the ellipse, a negative value is assigned to the major axis (a point to which we will return).

Together, these lines, here presented in the broadest strokes, form a mathematical order of their own, the so-called second order of mathematics, offering an array of other, significant traits. They are classified under the general heading of *conic sections*, because they can be represented as different ways of slicing a cone to obtain surfaces with distinct properties. These lines provide the basis for interesting symbolic representations. I will mention only one example, but all simple lines of the second order* are suitable for illustrating, to the senses, the abstract and general relations and proportions that prevail in a given, finite sphere.

* Only straight lines belong to the first order; with each higher order, the number of lines concerned grows disproportionately.

The hyperbola always possessed a ghostly quality in my eyes, although I could never figure out the reason why; later, I found the answer in a symbolic relation that can be posited for this figure, and I'm convinced that all other relations point to the same character. The matter must be viewed in connection with the other kinds of line.

The circle symbolizes self-love, or egoism, the ellipse the ideal of friendship, the parabola love for the infinite, or divine, and the hyperbola bitterest hatred.

Let one focal point stand for one soul, the rays extending to the perimeter its strivings and actions, and the bent rays the purpose animating outward-directed activity; for example, I can act partly for my own sake and partly for another's. If the rays from the focus represent active psychic pursuits, as per the symbol's inner meaning, the rays striking the focus from the perimeter must represent feelings and sensations that are experienced passively. Thus, when a ray from one focus to the periphery is bent toward the other focus, the feelings of the latter soul are induced by impulses and actions occurring in the former.

An absolute egoist acts only for his own sake: rays shoot out toward the periphery so that commensurate feelings and sensations, coming back, will affect his own soul; the egoist is completely self-contained; of the actions performed, nothing occurs in reference to another psyche. The ray from the midpoint of the circle is always sent back to its source.

The ellipse can be considered a circle with a midpoint that has split into two focal points. When two souls emerge from one that has divided in two, each exists in and through its counterpart; each of them is the soul of a friend and acts to rouse commensurate feelings and sensations; no matter what ray shoots out to the periphery, its further course will lead to the other focal point: thoughts and possessions pour back and forth; such souls display concern for the external world only insofar as outside phenomena allow each one to act upon and on behalf of the other; when reflected, all elliptical radii are equal to the major axis linking both focal points, or psyches; the souls cannot but think and feel in agreement with feelings and strivings that strengthen this bond. No "mine" and "yours" exist in the ellipse; whatever is, applies to both foci equally. There are other symbols for the ideal of friendship that are more beautiful, but none that is truer.

Now take the hyperbola. Immense hatred has rent the friends asunder; each has turned away from the other, wresting the focus away and keeping it for himself; the one wants nothing to do with his fellow, and they avoid each other in perpetuity; all the same, they remain tied together through the bond of enmity; the sentiment of each turns away at the mere sight of the other, yet they stand facing; the thoughts of each one recoil from the other, but the bent rays remain centered on the focal point the hated individual occupies. The major axis, which had been the bond uniting them in the ellipse, has become the opposite in the hyperbola, and the rays extending from one focus that once meant peace now mark difference.

The parabola is a sublime symbol, a symbol of love for an ideal, for God, for the supersensible—for all that is beautiful, great, and attainable only in infinity: the vision floating in spirit before the soul. All rays from the focus of the parabola run toward the other focus, which lies in the endless beyond; each impulse and every thought aims for this point; by the same token, but conversely, no ray can enter the soul without having come to be in the realm of infinity; all sentiment and feeling refer to this origin. The symbolism would be incomparably beautiful, were it possible to erect a house of worship with parabolic lines (which, admittedly, would remain open at one end because the parabola itself is not a closed figure), located at a site commensurate with its churchly dignity. Here, at the focus, would stand the altar or pulpit, so the priest would preside as the soul of the congregation, as it were; when he prayed, his prayer would echo into infinite, eternal mansions, and worshippers would behold a symbol of Eternal Voices converging at the inner sanctum of the church (focus), and illuminating the priest, whose inspired words would send them forth again.

There is no love for the absolutely diabolical. Indeed, the symbol for it is impossible ($y^2 = \sqrt{-px}$); it would have to be a parabola that turns away from the focal point lying in infinity and rushing toward its opposite, but mathematics shows that such a symbol cannot exist. Nothing in the world is worse than absolute egoism: self-love that relates all its actions to itself alone; all that the parabola does, it does without self-reference, for its every ray must traverse infinity before it can return to the initial point of focus; accordingly, the parabola is also the symbol of virtue, which acts for and on itself only by performing an action for All; the symbol of virtue coincides with the symbol of love for the divine.

Picture an infinitely great circle spanning the universe; it follows, since extremes always meet, and since all our symbols merge in vast endlessness, that this circle is simultaneously the symbol of the most absolute egoism and the most absolute love for others. God, as the midpoint of the Universal Circle, can only love Himself insofar as nothing outside Him exists: the periphery, or world, belongs to Him in essence, as body or matter; but in loving Himself, He at the same time loves all that *is*. Divine Love for Creation is a matter of self-preservation; God abides by loving all His creatures, which are but parts of the one and same infinite substance.

Extrema sese tangunt

Earlier, I advanced the thesis that if one pictures a straight line extending forever in opposite directions from a single source, their endpoints must be thought to intersect in infinity. But at first glance, it seems they should lie at an infinite remove from each other:

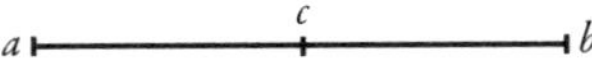

Thus, if one pictures *ca*, on the one hand, and *cb*, on the other, reaching out indefinitely, the endpoint *a* should ultimately coincide with endpoint *b*. Support for this paradoxical thesis, which is rich in implication for some of what follows, can be readily provided.

One should not think about a given line in terms of a single direction, but always bear at least two directions in mind; it is possible for two points to lie at an insuperable remove from each other in one sense, but to lie infinitely close, that is, to coincide, in the opposite sense. I will illustrate the matter with a bent line; the extent to which it can be applied to a straight one will be made clear in turn.

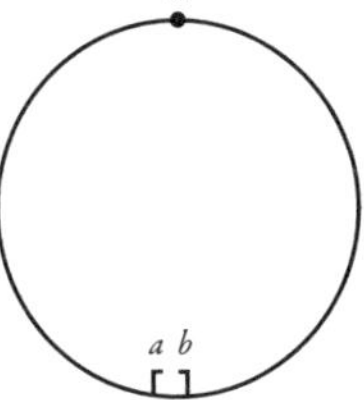

Let us assume we have a circular path, with two people—*a* and *b*—standing at point *d*; if both of them set out in opposite directions, along *da* and *db*, they will meet up where the figures shows them above—just as two people who set out in opposite directions from a point on the earth's surface at the same latitude eventually will cross paths. One might object that this statement is true only with regard to a curvilinear course—am I claiming that two people moving apart on a straight path will finally meet up? In infinity, they will. Make the circle above twice as big, and its curvature at each point is diminished by half; now make it as large as our planet's equator: the human eye cannot distinguish a section of this circle from a straight line; if the circle is infinitely large, it's impossible to distinguish any section—no matter how long—from a straight line; what has been said still holds: two people setting out in opposite directions along a curvilinear trajectory—which now is the same as a straight one—will meet again, if only in infinity. Thus, if we posit that I am actually following a straight path in space, and someone else is also doing so, from the same point but in the opposite direction, it is indifferent for mental representation whether I picture a given stage of progress as part of an infinitely large circle or as part of a straight line; I can be sure—provided that compassing infinity does not inspire terror—that I will see my friend again.

The matter admits demonstration in another way, too. For our visual organs and intellectual faculties alike, two points coincide when absolutely no space can be thought to extend between them; infinity does not exist for sensory perception, and so, if we are to speak of relations within infinity,* we must make

* If mathematicians may do so apropos of parallel lines, it is equally permissible in the case at hand.

our way in the purely conceptual realm. On a straight line, each point looks in two opposing directions. For instance, in this line,

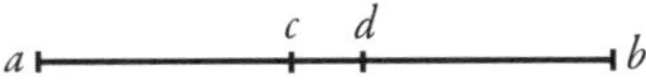

point *c* looks both toward *ca* and *cb*, as follows from our sensory intuition, the nature of the point itself, and the quality of the line. If *ca* and *cb* have traversed the universe, there can no longer be any spatial points beyond *ca* and *cb* in these directions (whereas infinitely many points exist between *a* and *b* in the directions of *bc* and *ac*); anything beyond them would have to have been covered, as well; since the very concept of coincidence declares it impossible that a point be thought separating *a* and *b* in the directions *ca* and *cb*, they must coincide in one direction and stand infinitely far apart in the opposite direction. The same basic conditions hold for the points *c* and *d* in the line. In the directions *cd* and *dc*, they are immediately adjacent, and in the directions *ca* and *db*, an infinite distance separates them; therefore, in our own world, one can view any given point as the coincidence of two straight lines extending from opposite points at an immeasurable distance. Accordingly, a finite circle is just the finite image of an infinitely straight line; by the same token, a straight, finite line is just a fragment of an infinitely great ring, and linear extension means striving to join with, and become, this boundless circle.

Mathematics provides striking confirmation for this thesis in its formulization of the hyperbola and ellipse. The formula for the latter, with the abscissas measured from the origin of the major axis, is familiar enough: $y^2 = px - \frac{px^2}{2a}$.

Take the major axis in the negative, so that all relations hold in reverse, and an ellipse becomes a hyperbola:

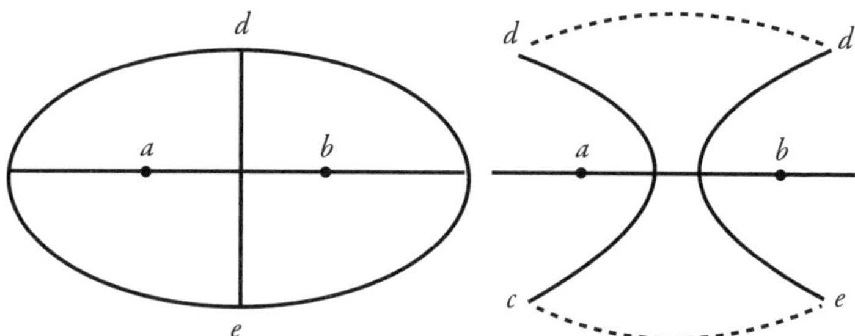

Here, the halves *a* and *b*, instead of turning in concave manner, as in the ellipse, assume convex form; the points *d* and *e* will only meet up in infinity—but they must, since the equation for the hyperbola is the same as that for the continuous ellipse, except that the substitution of a negative sign for a positive one entails convergence in the opposite direction; hence the hyperbola's spidery legs.

This, incidentally, is not the only support that mathematics offers; other evidence abounds, all of which is granted validity by the general proposition that any given value can pass into its opposite both through infinity and through zero.

As visible confirmation one might also take the familiar phenomenon of catoptrics. If a light source is placed on the axis of a hollow mirror at a sizeable remove from its surface, all the rays of the same will be reflected back into the main focus of the mirror and the image of the light will appear at this point. If the light source is brought closer to the mirror, the image previously appearing at the main focus will move farther away from the mirror's surface and closer to the midpoint of the mirror's curvature, which lies at twice the distance, on the axis, of the main focus from its surface. As the light reaches the midpoint of the curvature itself, it coincides with the image—now also reflected toward this same point. If the light is brought still closer, the image, increasing in size, passes beyond the midpoint so that the light now occupies a space between its image and the mirror. Thus, the closer the light comes from the midpoint of the curvature toward the main focus, the farther away its image moves; when the light reaches the main focus itself, it falls at an infinite remove and can no longer be seen at all. If, now, the light is brought even closer to the mirror's surface so it stands between it and the main focus, the image will reappear—but in the opposite direction. Initially, it will appear very far away and large, growing smaller the closer it is brought to the mirror's surface, where it will again coincide with its image.—Obviously, if the light stood at the main focal point, its image—were the human eye able to attain infinity—would be visible in either direction, since the point it occupied would mark the outer limit in both directions, where they finally meet.

ATTEMPT TO DEVELOP ORGANIC LAW FROM SPATIAL SYMBOLISM

The essence of a given organism is a multiplicity of parts that constitute a strict unity. Strictly speaking, then, there is no spatial symbol more appropriate than the point for illustrating an organism's functions: a point is something indivisible and wholly in agreement with itself, fusing all the varied qualities one might imagine. Just as one can picture the whole weight of a stone unified in a single point—the center of gravity—one can posit the same for every organism: the soul; as is the case for a stone, an organism's center of gravity does not exist in and of itself but as an ideal bringing together material parts.

It follows that the point does not, in fact, provide a complete symbol of the organism; by essence, the organism is not just unity but also a plurality.

Now picture the point, which we have posited as a symbol of organic unity, as the most intensive form of something reaching to all sides, in the process becoming a circle.* This circle perfectly symbolizes each and every organic entity; alternatively, whatever is organic admits symbolization as a circle (which, of course, means discounting all the particular relations characteristic of specific organisms). The circle is the symbol only for the most general of organic relations: what is found in the circle can be found in every

* In truth, a sphere; but for the sake of simplicity, it will be viewed as a circle here.

organism, but not the other way around. However, particular organisms are simply different stages of development of the same symbol, or fragments of a specific stage of development. In the symbol's further evolution (as we will see below), the form of particular organisms would occur as a matter of course, such that one would have, in the development of the symbol, that of the organisms themselves.

In the first stage of the symbol's evolution toward the circle, the point, symbolizing unity, actually represents the central node of infinite multiplicity: the points of the periphery, which can be considered to depend on it. We can enlist an example ready at hand, the human body, to illustrate the inherent symbolism. (Needless to say, preliminary familiarity with the same must be presumed to understand the matter.) The developmental scheme can be demonstrated on the basis of systems or organs; I will use the former in the following.

All the functions of the human body constitute a perfect unity; each function cooperates in the workings of the others and itself exists through their cooperation; in turn, each basic system is contained within the others, which help to constitute it: vessels and nerves in the membranes, membranes and vessels in the nerves, membranes and nerves in the vessels; accordingly, we can picture that all functions perform their operations at a single point—that the vascular, nervous, and skin systems are fused into one.

But just as soon, intension transforms into extension as the point expands in linear fashion to all sides, becoming a circle. Were it possible for the point to expand unimpeded, it would come to fill the universe—which it still strives to do, by virtue of the inertia that inheres in all organic motion; in fact, our point must be viewed as a site surrounded by a much greater periphery, which is the external world, and as soon as it starts expanding outward, the latter coalesces to push it back. This struggle of the point—seeking to expand *ad infinitum* and the periphery contracting and counteracting it—symbolizes life.

To be dead is to be identical, and to be identical is to remain fused with the external world, as is every point until it awakens to life by entering into opposition and grappling with the great periphery that surrounds it, the world outside. Hereby, the point becomes a circle, running in radial form up against it, just as it pushes back from the opposite direction; where the twain meet there arises a boundary between the organic-living and the external world, to which the circle formerly belonged but from which it now emerges, individualized and independent; the periphery is the site where interaction occurs between the organism and the external world, which then is propagated by both.

There are three principal aspects to be observed in the circle: the center, or unity; the periphery, or infinite plurality; and that which connects unity and plurality, the radius, extending from the center to the periphery and back from the periphery to the center; each aspect exists through the two other aspects. By essence and in the most general sense of the relations that define it, each and every organism constitutes a trinity.

Take the sphere of the nervous system as the center, from where every dynamic impulse proceeds; the sphere of the skin- or cell system* represents the periphery, bordering the external world and engaged in material exchanges with it; the sphere of the

* The skin is to be viewed as an enlarged cell, or the cell as miniaturized skin, and everywhere the cell system takes the form of husks or skins and forms their basis; therefore I prefer to call the cell system viewed as a whole, precisely because it is a system, the skin system.

vascular system is the totality of radii receiving stimuli from inside to outside through the nervous system, and matter passing from outside to inside through the vegetative system of the membranes. If you wish, the nervous system represents the function of sensation, the vascular system that of irritation/inflammation, and the cell or skin system the vegetative function; without the underlying connections, these names are just words: The Trinity is at work here, too. In part the nervous system exists only inasmuch as it affects the vascular and skin systems, from which it is affected in turn—just as the midpoint of a circle is a dynamic presence only in relation to radii and peripheral points. Likewise, in part the vascular system could not be active if it did not receive its dynamic impetus from the nervous system, on the one hand, and material from cells and skin (e.g., intestinal lining, pleura), on the other. Finally, the skin and cells must partly be provided by the vessels with what they secrete. None of the three basic systems can operate, or exist in the first place, without the others. By nature, radii presuppose a midpoint, and their limit points form a periphery on their own; the midpoint exists only insofar as its radii extend to a periphery and, from there, reach back to it; a periphery exists only as the border line of radii reaching out from a center. Thus, in the animal kingdom as in the development of the fetus, the vascular system, nervous system, and skin system depend on, and exist through, each other simultaneously.

Just by the form we see how the symbol has been followed in general. The nervous system is constructed as a series of points, the vascular system displays a linear arrangement, and the skin system takes the shape of cells or tubes. At the first level of symbolic development, the skin is a single cell enveloping the whole.

In turn, intermediate systems emerge, whose place within the symbol follows as a matter of course as the basic systems pass into each other; when viewed in isolation, the division therefore already appears artificial and somewhat forced.

The muscle system, insofar as it passes into the vascular system (heart, *tunica muscularis*) is a latent presence at the border between the vascular and nervous systems, an intermediary fusing both, or is expressed by the points that immediately surround the center and melt with it into one, from which the radius passes outward in one direction and, conversely, strikes the midpoint in the other; therefore, all activity of the nervous system shifts over to the muscle system, and arteries can perform their function only because of their muscular component. The heart belongs to this same, central musculature.

Up to this account of the muscle system, I have left aside a division that can also be made apropos of the vascular system. In the vascular system, two directions are to be distinguished: the arterial and the venous. The ray extending from the central muscle is the *artery*, and the totality of such rays the arterial system; on a divergent course, they run from one point to all parts of the organism, from inside to outside. In contrast, the rays from the periphery—the skin system—head toward the center and originate in effects produced by the external, material world; they reach into the organism through the convergent lines represented by the *venous system*. By nature, arteries are muscular; they stem from the central muscle and can be viewed as its continuation; the vein is membranous and only becomes muscular where it finally joins the central muscle. Artery walls are flexible, because they receive impulses from the center point, or nervous system, through the muscle system that surrounds it. The substance in the veins—blood—is mobile, but not the wall belonging to the organism itself; venous walls never receive impulses, but the blood does, and conveys their motion from the periphery toward the center. At the periphery, in the skin or cell tissue, arterial and venous paths merge; here, arteries turn into veins, the inverse of their convergence in the central muscle.

The skin also contains (in a broader sense than the anatomic structure described above) the beginning of the venous system and the ending of the arterial one, in the form of lymphatic (absorbent) and exhalant vessels. The exhalant vessel is symbolized by a point where the ray running outward—the artery—strikes the periphery and coincides with it, and the absorbent vessel by the point where a ray running back from the periphery starts. Such points are what constitute the periphery in the first place; in essence, the entirety of the skin- or cell system comprises so many absorbent and exhalant vessels, and by virtue of this alone is it able to effect exchanges with the external world.

Lymphatic and exhalant vessels do not really form an intermediary system between the skin and vascular systems; rather, they comprise the vascular system itself, as it passes over into the skin.

The actual intermediary system between the skin system and the vascular system is constituted by the paths of digestion, breathing, and urination, which are membranes shaped like vessels that run throughout the whole body; the vascular system draws from them and discharges excreted matter into them. Symbolically, they may be viewed as follows.

Picture the periphery divided into two rows of points lying next to each other, an outer row and an inner one. With its outward-facing, convex side, the first represents the outer layer of skin; the other side, which is immediately connected but concave and facing inward, represents a mucous membrane. Likewise, on the second row of peripheral points, a convex side turned toward the mucous membrane and a concave side turned inward are to be distinguished: the first represents the muscle tissue of the intestines (the genesis of which will soon be discussed), and the second the system of *serous membranes*. If we consider these adjacent peripheries to form a thin ring constituted by mucous membranes, muscle tissue, and serous membranes, we have a hint of the body's vegetative system.

Muscle tissue, it seems, extends into the intestines along with the arteries until it reaches the periphery; indeed, as has been shown empirically, it grows stronger in proportion to the further arterial course, so that, at the latter's outer limit, its *lumen* disappears altogether by condensing into compact muscular mass. Here, at the periphery, the artery sloughs off this tissue, which now takes on the qualities of dermal tissue, muscle tissue in the intestines, and perhaps the skin muscle of animals; the remaining arterial tissue dissolves into other tissues, as exhalant vessels.—That said, the whole matter is not entirely clear to me.

The skin system borders not only the vascular system within, forming with it an intermediary system, but also the external world—which qualifies as inorganic, relative to the organism itself—and merges with it to make (another) intermediary system, that of the epidermis. The epidermis is half-organic and half-inorganic, fitted to the environment in which the organism finds itself—hence the calcareous exterior of the egg, the exoskeleton of lower animals, horn-like excrescences, scales, feathers, and the tough outer layer of skin in human beings.

The skin system and the nerve system do not combine into an intermediary system because the radius, or vascular system, lies between them; unless, as one can also do, one views the latter as the intermediary system. Incidentally, the skin system must also have nerves, for it surrounds the midpoint—that is, the nervous system—as a covering; in my eyes, the fact that a neural node forms at the center of each particular cell has a symbolic basis.

The nervous system pervades everything; the vascular system reaches everywhere; and the skin system surrounds it all. If one views the center as a small circle, then this symbol already points toward assorted nerve masses, although the borders of the same, marked by neighboring systems, remain obscure to me. I will explore the matter more fully at a later date. For the time being, I would simply observe that the symbol can be applied to the world as such, which, in light of general relations that prevail here (and provided that one accepts the thesis advanced in the previous section) qualifies as an organism in its own right.

Were one to declare that the beginning (the egg) of the world was a point—a point of utmost intensity—this would symbolize nothing more than the agreement of all things in perfect unity; the multiplicity of what the world *is*, the means by which the world finds expression, would not yet be manifest. But now, we can see the point expand: intension turns into extension; inasmuch as there is nothing outside the point to restrict it, it stretches into infinity—which we can imagine only in terms of finite schemata (a measure that can hardly be avoided in most cases, anyway). Only when each of the rays has run to infinity does it meet up with another ray headed in the opposite direction; instead of a finite organism being contained by the surrounding, external world, the infinite organism encounters its other half; together they form their own antithesis. Along these lines, the equation for the finite can be carried over to the infinite.

In response to the question of what this symbol means, I affirm: the midpoint is God, the Animating Principle of the World-whole, existing in pure ideality—or, in other words, the General, the Absolute, from which all that is particular must be thought to proceed and depend. The infinite ray is linear time stretching forth boundlessly, in which all particular beings take on individual shape, out of the General and Absolute. But this ray reaches in a twofold direction. Extending from the center to the infinite periphery, it is the process of time's becoming. Likewise, but conversely, as the ray goes from the periphery to the center, it is the passing of time. The indifference point, where both directions merge in infinity, is presence: the infinite periphery of space encompassing all that exists. The present is the momentary coincidence of passing and becoming, and life a constant evolution in time, emergence from and return to generality through the circulation of the world, whereby what is taken away comes forth anew. Reality and interaction occur only at the periphery: what stands before it has not yet been and is only now in the course of development, and what stands behind it (or, more precisely, what occurs in the sense of the opposing ray) has already been. A perpetual cycle governs the world, a serpent biting its tail in all directions. Here, we can take any given point as the center of an infinite periphery (*mundus est sphaera, cujus centrum ubique, peripheria nusquam*), just as it may be considered to occupy the periphery of a center at an infinite remove. Each and every point in the world has this twofold orientation, deeming itself the center around which the external world revolves, while being but a part in service to a still-greater periphery. As the midpoint is located everywhere in an infinite sphere, so is God all places at once, at the innermost core of each of His creatures. In human beings, reason is the divine share, the root and anchor of Being.

The next level of the symbol presents greater difficulty, because matters get much more complicated. I admit that here—and even at the first level of symbolic development—not everything is clear.

That said, I will set down what has become plain to me; at the very least, it will suffice to show how, through the ongoing force of one and the same law, the diversity manifest in the organism might come into existence.

Let us assume, then—the extent to which it is valid to do so and how our thesis derives from the lawful development of the first symbol must be elaborated at a later date—that the organism becomes an ellipse through a splitting of the midpoint in opposite directions in the course of forming a circle (if not in some other way).

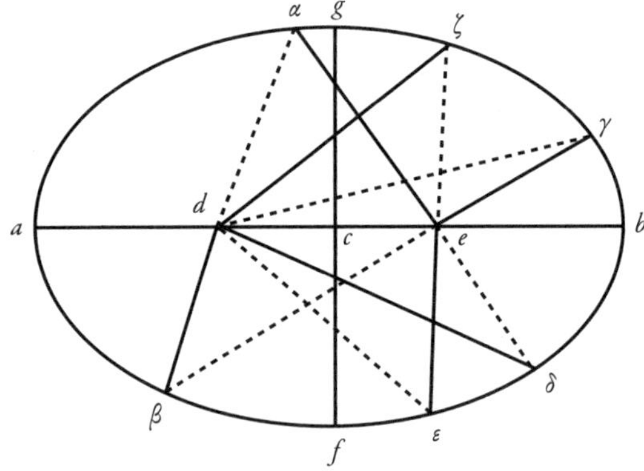

The point that has remained in the middle, *c*, and the two diverging branches *cd* and *ce*, represent the nervous system in an ulterior state of development. The midpoint, *c*, stands for the central organs of the same, and the other sections of the major axis *da* and *eb* represent the independent muscle system, which emerges where the vascular and nervous systems overlap. The foci represent the heart: *d* the left, and *a* the right side, in each of which the ventricles and atrium are still fused; the rays issuing from the foci and going back to them are those of the vascular system. The muscles *da*

and *eb* are, in fact, also vessels, except that they contain nerve mass, not blood. Their point of origin is the heart, where one part of the arterial endings condenses into muscle tissue, as far as I can see. At the same time, they join the skin as cutaneous tissue in mammals and a bonelike covering that approximates the skin in lower animals. (I confess this point is not yet altogether clear.) The periphery is the skin system as a whole, which contains all subsystems: epidermis (or exoskeleton), intestinal tract, lungs, and assorted cell membranes.

When, from the left heart, *d*, a ray extends toward the periphery—*dδ* or *dβ* or *dζ*, etc.—it symbolizes the aorta system, which extends to the surface of the skin and cell tissue throughout the body. Where it comes to interact with external substances, it is bent back* as the convergent system of the *vena cava* toward the other focal point: the right heart, *e*. Consequently, all rays—*δe*, *βe*, *ζe*, etc.—belong to this system. Now, from focus *b*, the ray sets out again in the directions *eα*, *eσ*, *eγ*, etc., as the pulmonary artery—for the lung is still fused with the skin at the periphery (as comparative anatomy proves)—then interacts with the external world once more, and runs back as the pulmonary vein *αd*, *σd*, *γd*, etc., to the left heart, whereupon the cycle begins anew. According to this scheme, only the aorta and the *arteria pulmonalis* are muscular extensions of the heart; the *vena cava* and *vena pulmonalis* are extensions of the skin. The meaning of the minor axis is not entirely clear to me yet—it would seem merely to represent the dividing line between the right and left halves of the body.

* For brevity's sake, we can keep this expression, but it is not entirely accurate to speak of a ray being "bent back" when discussing symbolic evolution, for the counteraction of the external world is what brings about movement toward the other focus.

In fact, the ellipse represents an organic part of the second level of developmental organization. For reasons to be provided anon, one should picture every ray of the first, circular level of development as an ellipse—just as curved lines on the surface of the water appear to be intertwined without interfering with each other.

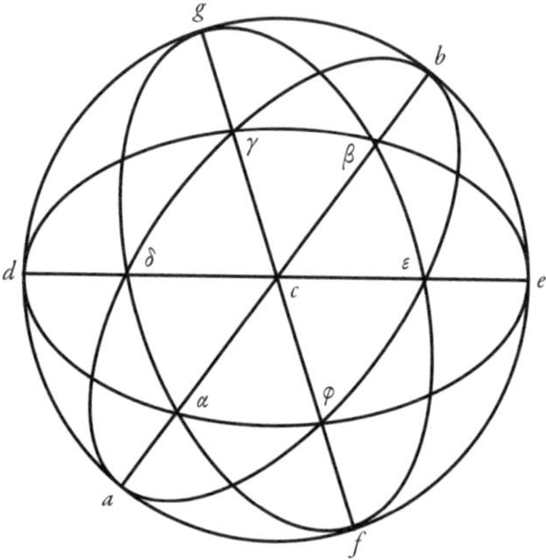

This is the case in the figure above, where the three rays *ab*, *de*, and *gf* are represented accordingly and the respective foci of the ellipses diagrammed are the points *α* and *β*, *δ*, and *ε*, *γ*, and *φ*. All emergent ellipses are then delimited by the general circumference *adgbef*, which represents outer integuments pure and simple; the other skin systems in the elliptical periphery are already moving inward. It is not difficult to understand that, if one pictures all rays of the first symbol as having evolved into ellipses, then the foci *α*, *δ*, *γ*, and so on become innumerable and make a circle of their own. Therefore, at the second, full level of symbolic development, the heart still forms a closed ring; in a sun-like pattern, the rays of the nervous system expand toward it on all sides: as *cα*, *cβ*, *cγ*, *cδ*, and so on.

That the ellipse must emerge in the second stage of organic symbolic development is perfectly clear. The mechanism by which this occurs is fairly clear, too—even though much about it is still obscure and will remain so until I can make further advances in the mechanical sciences, on the basis of which I hope to offer greater insights. Thus, I am still unable to provide a sure reason why the various ellipses should not interfere with each other. That such interference need not occur is evident, at very least, when liquid media stand at issue; in principle, the matter should be brought to bear on symbolic evolution: after all, an egg contains only liquid. Anyway, and as already remarked, further investigation is required. The law of symbolic development—however unequal to the task I may yet be—seems to amount to the following.

Each and every organism, over and over and *in toto*, obeys the same principle. When a stone is cast, it travels, thanks to its inertia, in one and the same direction. A similar law of inertia holds for organic development: the same law underlying the evolution of a point into a circle governs each point of the newly emergent circle, making it expand and assume this shape; in the new circle, it exercises the same effect on each particular point, and so on, so that the process keeps going. Indeed, it would continue *ad infinitum* (just as our stone would keep flying forever), were it not that every organism is incorporated into a higher organism that keeps it from continuing unimpeded and, by exercising a counterforce, allows it to take shape only to a certain degree. Likewise, when thrown on the earth's surface, a stone can reach only a certain height; when it has reached its *acme*, it falls again, because it is subject to the gravitational pull of the earth. But the World-organism itself, which really does extend infinitely, shows that such unlimited evolution is, in itself, possible.

To get an approximate idea—albeit one that will require immediate modification—consider the following figure:

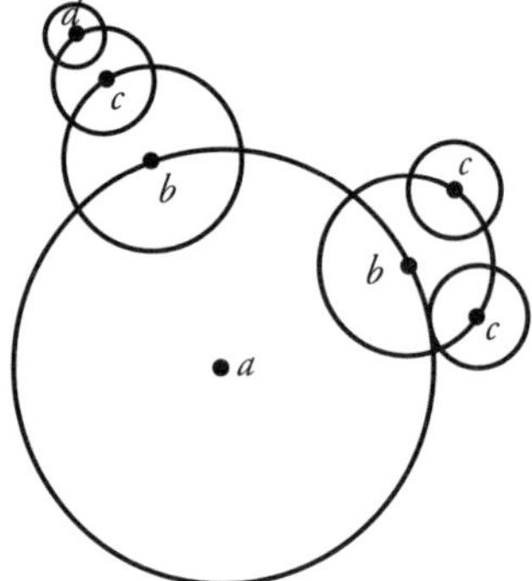

Each peripheral point, *b*, that one can imagine issuing from *a* will, in turn, bring forth its own peripheries, and any given point, *c*, will represent the midpoint of new circles. And so on, and so forth.

According to this scheme, symbolic development would not seem to pose any particularly great difficulty. At the same time, however, it is impossible for the circle to develop into lines of a higher order, or just ellipses, in this manner. One item has been neglected, which introduces enormous modifications to the Symbol. To wit, our figure shows, in rough form, how the Symbol would develop if, once the circle has expanded to periphery *b*, the midpoint were to remain dead and inert; only now would each point *b* begin to expand to a certain periphery, *c*, then rest, and each point *c* calmly expand on its own. But this is not the case. In the ongoing expansion of point *a*, whereby *b* emerges from it, *b*—and then *c*, too—immediately starts expanding, so that all these motions are in fact concurrent.

To begin with, let us consider just two points, *b* and *b′*, in the periphery produced by *a*, located at the opposing ends of a radius of the same.

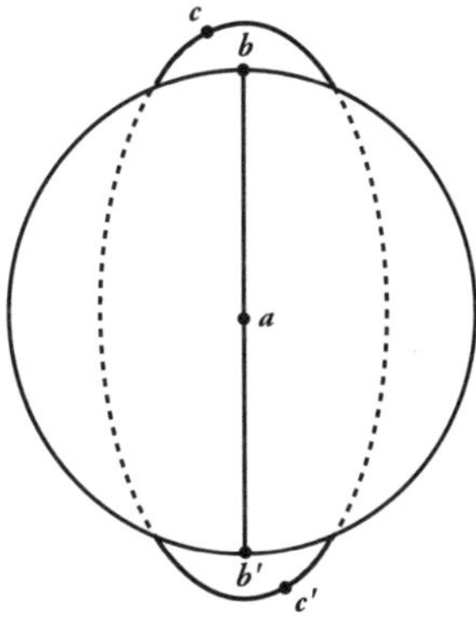

As these points in the periphery around *a* start to expand into circles of their own, the expansive effect of *a* continues to act; that is, they are driven forward, in the process of forming circles, along the radial lines *ab* and *ab'*. Now, the linear motion conferred by *a* combines with their independent expansion, such that the circular shape they would form, if *a* were to rest, would stretch out lengthwise. No sensible figure could emerge, if *b* and *b'* started to expand on their own only after gaining distance from *a* through the latter's expansion. The law of constancy governing organic development demands that, as soon as the points *b* and *b'* have emerged from *a*—already forming a periphery but still infinitely proximate to *a*—they begin to make circles of their own. Then, the more *b* and *b'* gain distance from *a* (in its own course of expansion), the more they are drawn out lengthwise until they merge at *a*, from which they reemerge in the opposite direction, making an ellipse with the focal points *b* and *b'*—the original, opposing positions in the periphery of *a*. In fact, points *b* and *b'* are to be viewed as having emerged in the first place through the process of *a* splitting apart in opposite directions in the course of forming a circle. That said, the innate striving to develop in circular form does not concern just points *b* and *b'* (as illustrated above), but all other points peripheral to *a*

that one can imagine, from which it follows that the intersection of resultant ellipses must occur (as also indicated in the diagram).

I will not elaborate on this Symbol—in part because, as previously mentioned, I still consider myself ill-equipped to address a problem that, to be solved, will require all the resources of higher analysis properly applied to mechanics, and in part because the application of the Symbol presupposes thoroughgoing knowledge of comparative anatomy and natural history, with which I have managed to date only to acquire passing familiarity. Meanwhile, I defer further discussion until a propaedeutic fundament has been achieved. At any rate, ulterior symbolic evolution occurs through the continued effect of the same law: The points of the elliptical circumference expand, each on its own, into circles, and so on, but the motion implanted in them persists concurrently with their independent development.

The movements of heavenly bodies admit being boiled down to the same, simple law. Throughout, one must not forget that everything set forth here has been said about just one section of the True Symbol, of which the sphere represents the lowest level and the highest—as I have reason to believe—is once again a sphere, albeit one not to be found on our earth. Furthermore, I believe to have found grounds, however inadequate they remain for the time being, on the basis of which it may be concluded that if symbolic development is not halted at the point of elliptical coincidence, but proceeds so that the ellipses evolve for their own part, not infinitely many, but just three developing ellipses may be presumed on the plane of intersection.—Here, for the Infinite Organism, parabolas take their place.

Erik Butler has translated dozens of books from modern European languages, many of them for Wakefield Press. He is currently at work on a study of self-taught eccentric Jean-Pierre Brisset (1837–1919), who traced human language and origins back to frogs.